THERE SHALL BE NO NIGHT

BY

ROBERT E. SHERWOOD

NEW YORK

CHARLES SCRIBNER'S SONS

1940

THIS PLAY IS DEDICATED

WITH MY LOVE

TO MY WIFE

MADELINE

"There Shall Be No Night" was produced and presented by The Playwrights' Company—Maxwell Anderson, S. N. Behrman, Elmer Rice, Robert E. Sherwood—and The Theatre Guild—for the first time at the Opera House in Providence, R. I., on March 29th, 1940, with the following cast:

DR. KAARLO VALKONEN . . . . Alfred Lunt

MIRANDA VALKONEN . . . . Lynn Fontanne

DAVE CORWEEN . . . . Richard Whorf

UNCLE WALDEMAR . . . . Sydney Greenstreet

GUS SHUMAN . . . . Brooks West

ERIK VALKONEN . . . . Montgomery Clift

KAATRI ALQUIST . . . . Elisabeth Fraser

DR. ZIEMSSEN . . . . Maurice Colbourne

MAJOR RUTKOWSKI . . . . Edward Raquello

JOE BURNETT . . . . Charles Ansley

BEN GICHNER . . . . Thomas Gomez

FRANK OLMSTEAD . . . . William Le Massena

SERGEANT GOSDEN . . . . Claude Horton

LEMPI . . . . Phyllis Thaxter

ILMA . . . . Charva Chester

PHOTOGRAPHER . . . . Ralph Nelson

PHOTOGRAPHER . . . . Robert Downing

Staged by Alfred Lunt.

Settings designed by Richard Whorf.

vii

THERE SHALL BE NO NIGHT

SCENES

PREFACE

After the first performance of "There Shall Be No Night" in Providence, Rhode Island, on March 29, 1940, a young man, a stranger, came up to me and said, "You certainly have changed your point of view since 'Idiot's Delight.' " There was a distinct note of accusation in his voice. This was the first of many similar and many less temperate accusations which this play has provoked. Having identified myself time and again in the past as a pacifist, I had now become a "Warmonger."

It is a strange fact that many people who can bear with equanimity all sorts of assaults upon their moral character or their personal habits are goaded to indignant counter-attack when they are charged with inconsistency. "I don't mind being called a black-hearted villain, an enemy of society. In fact, I might even be flattered by such distinction. But—by God—I'll fight any man who dares to imply that I have been untrue to myself."

Therefore, I wish to preface this play with a review of the development of my own point of view, as it has been expressed in other plays. I want to say that "There Shall Be No Night" is not a denial of "Idiot's Delight": it is a sequel. I realize that there is an appreciable difference be-

tween what I have written and what I have tried
to write. But I shall deal in this Preface with my
motives, and the nature of the experience which
impelled them.

As a common soldier in the Canadian army in
the first World War, in training camps, in the
line, in hospitals, and in clinks, I was mixed in
with men from all over the British Empire and the
United States. In one hospital the occupant of the
bed on one side of mine was an Australian who
had been horribly burned by liquid fire in the
crater at Loos three years before. In the bed on
the other side of mine was a South African Jew;
a machine gun bullet had lodged in the base of his
spine and he knew he would never walk again. It
was a great surprise to me to discover that these
two men, and all other men whom I got to know
well, thought and talked and acted and reacted
just about as I did. What was so surprising about
it was the revelation of the narrowness and shal-
lowness of my own mind. I had been brought up
to believe that because I was a 100 per cent American—and a Harvard man, at that—I was superior.

At the age of twenty-two my career as a soldier was ended—for all time, as I then hopefully
believed. I became a veteran, and as such recap-
tured a certain sense of superiority. (That didn't
last long, either. Never was there a baser decep-
tion than the famous recruiting poster which
showed a cute little girl pointing a chubby finger

at her father and asking, "Daddy—what did YOU do in the Great War?" As things have turned out, when the children of my generation point the finger at us the one word that follows it is "Sucker!") I took with me out of the army certain convictions, which have stayed with me and which all the dreadful events of the past twenty years have served only to strengthen.

I became internationally minded—and in the opinion of the apostles of isolationism, the word "internationalist" is synonymous with "warmonger." I believed that war was a hideous injustice and that no man had the right to call himself civilized as long as he admitted that another world war could conceivably be justifiable. I believed that the beginning of the elimination of war was the elimination of nationalism, the chauvinistic concept of patriotism. And I believed that the beginning of the elimination of nationalism was in some form of union of the English-speaking peoples who were already united by the advantages of a common language, common traditions of freedom, common ethics, and a common desire for peace.

I was instinctively enthusiastic about the scheme for a League of Nations. I wanted to believe that there would be some medium for expressing the good will that I shared with the scalded Australian and the paralyzed South African Jew. But, in 1919, I was convinced of the futility of the League by the writings of George Harvey and

other Wilson-haters. I became a rabid opponent
of the League—which means that whenever I engaged in a discussion of the major political issues
in some speak-easy I would say "The League
won't work because it's impractical. I agree abso-
lutely with Senator Henry Cabot Lodge that
Article XVI stinks!" I had a very hazy idea of
what Article XVI actually provided for, but I
was young and free again and it was much more
fun to be a critic than an adherent.

In 1920, I confess with deep shame, my first
vote as an American citizen was cast for Warren
G. Harding. Thus, I did my bit in the great betrayal. I voted for the proposition that all the
American soldiers who had given their lives in the
Great War had died in vain. And what I and
all other Americans got from Harding's victory
was a decade of hypocrisy, corruption, crime,
glorification of greed and depravity, to be followed logically by a decade of ascendant Hitlerism.

In 1926 I wrote my first play. My main reason
for doing so was that I was about to be thirty
years old, and I had read somewhere—I think it
was in F.P.A.'s column—that all young news-
papermen promise themselves that they will write
that play or that novel before they're thirty and
then the next thing they know they're forty and
still promising. I didn't have time for a novel.
When I wrote "The Road to Rome" I didn't know
what sort of playwright I might be, provided I

might be a playwright at all. So I tried in it
every style of dramaturgy—high comedy, low
comedy, melodrama, romance (both sacred and
profane), hard-boiled realism, beautiful writing—
and, of course, I inserted a "message." That
message was that I was opposed to war. But any
one who remembers "The Road to Rome" remembers it principally for one line, which came near
the end of the play. Hannibal, the Carthaginian
conqueror, having spent a night with Amytis, the
wife of the Roman dictator, Fabius Maximus, has
been persuaded by that pleasant experience to
spare Rome from destruction. When Hannibal is
about to retreat from the Eternal City, the following dialogue occurs:

HANNIBAL

Fabius, I wish happiness and prosperity to you,
your wife, and your sons.

FABIUS

Thank you—but I have no sons.

HANNIBAL

You may have . . .

After "The Road to Rome" I made several un-
successful attempts to repeat the same formula:
"a modern comedy in ancient dress." Chief of
these was a play (unproduced) called "Marching

As To War." The scene of this was England in the reign of Richard the Lion-hearted and the hero of it was a conscientious objector who refused to go on the Crusade.

In October, 1929—while Prime Minister Ramsay MacDonald was visiting President Herbert Hoover, offering "Faith, Hope and Parity," and Wall Street was just getting ready to crash—I tried another kind of play, "Waterloo Bridge," which was written from my own observations of blacked out, hungry London in 1917. The most important speech in this was spoken by a Canadian soldier. He has just emerged from hospital —an air-raid is going on—and his girl tells him he must go back to France and fight the war. He says:

"Yes—fight the war. What's the war, anyway? It's that guy up there in his aeroplane. What do I care about him and his bombs? What do I care who he is, or what he does, or what happens to him? That war's over for me. What I've got to fight is the whole dirty world. That's the enemy that's against you and me . . ."

"Waterloo Bridge" was almost good. But it was incoherent. Two years after it, I wrote "Reunion in Vienna." I went into this play with what seemed to me an important if not strikingly original idea —science hoist with its own petard—and came out with a gay, romantic comedy. But in the Preface to that play I came closer than I ever had before to a statement of what I was trying to think and write. I quote at length from this Preface, because it has a considerable bearing on all that I have written since then:

"This play is another demonstration of the escape mechanism in operation.

"There is no form of mechanism more popular or in more general use in this obstreperously technological period—which is a sufficient indication of the spirit of moral defeatism that now prevails. It is a spirit, or want of spirit, that can truthfully be said to be new in the world—for the reason that in no previous historic emergency has the common man enjoyed the dubious advantages of consciousness. However unwillingly, he is now able to realize that his generation has the ill-luck to occupy the limbo-like interlude between one age and another. Looking about him, he sees a shell-torn No Man's Land, filled with barbed-wire entanglements and stench and uncertainty. If it is not actual chaos, it is a convincing counterfeit thereof. Before him is black doubt, punctured by brief flashes of ominous light, whose revelations are not comforting. Behind him is nothing but the ghastly wreckage of burned bridges.

"In his desperation, which he assures himself is essentially comic, he casts about for weapons of defense. The old minds offer him Superstition, but it is a stringless bow, impotent in its obsolescence. The new minds offer him Rationalism, but it is a boomerang. He must devise pitiful defenses of his own, like a soldier who spreads a sheet of

wrapping paper over his bivouac to keep out the
airplane bombs. In Europe, this manifests itself
in the heroic but anachronistic attempt to recre-
ate the illusions of nationalism: people drugging
themselves with the comforting hope that tomorrow will be a repetition of yesterday, that the
Cæsars and the Tudors will return.

"In America, which has had no Cæsars or Tudors, nor even any Hohenzollerns or Habsburgs,
the favorite weapon of defense against unlovely
reality is a kind of half-hearted cynicism that is
increasingly tremulous, increasingly shrill. . . .

"Democracy—liberty, equality, fraternity, and
the pursuit of happiness! Peace and prosperity!
Emancipation by enlightenment! All the distilla-
tions of man's maturing intelligence have gone
sour.

"The worst of it is that man had been so full
of hope. He had complete confidence in the age of
reason, the age of the neutralization of nature,
for it was his own idea. It differed from all previous ages in this great respect: it was not caused
by the movements of glaciers, the upheaval or sub-
mersion of continents, the imposition of prolonged
droughts: it was the product of man's restless
thought and tireless industry, planned and developed by him not in collaboration with nature
but in implacable opposition to it. The reasonings
of such as Roger Bacon, Copernicus, Galileo and
Newton started the assault upon ignorance, and
it has been carried on by countless thinkers and

talkers from Voltaire and Rousseau to Shaw and
Wells.

"This is the career of the age of reason:

"The eighteenth century knew the excitements
of conception, culminating in the supreme orgasm
of the French Revolution.

"The nineteenth century was the period of ges-
tation, marred by occasional symptoms of nausea
and hysteria and a few dark forebodings, but gen-
erally orderly and complacent.

"For the twentieth century have remained the
excruciating labor pains and the discovery that
the child is a monster; and as modern man looks
upon it, and recalls the assurances of the omnis-
cient obstetricians, he is sore distressed. He wishes
that with his eyes he could see not, that with his
ears he could not hear. But his senses are remarkably acute. . . .

"Man is, for the moment, scornful of the for-
mulæ of the scientists, for he believes that it was
they who got him into this mess. To hell with
them, and their infallible laws, their experiments
noble in motive and disastrous in result, their anti-
septic Utopia, their vitamines and their lethal
gases, their cosmic rays and their neuroses, all
tidily encased in cellophane. To hell with them,
says man, but with no relish, for he has been deprived even of faith in the potency of damna-
tion. . . .

"So man is giving loud expression to his reluctance to confront the seemingly inevitable. He is

desperately cherishing the only remaining manifestation of the individualism which first distinguished him in the animal kingdom: it is the anarchistic impulse, rigorously inhibited but still alive—the impulse to be drunk and disorderly, to smash laws and ikons, to draw a mustache and beard on the Mona Lisa, to be a hurler of bombs and monkey wrenches—the impulse to be an artist and a damned fool. It was this impulse which animated Galileo in the face of Romanism and Lenin in the face of Tsarism, but the disciples of both of them are determined to exterminate it and can undoubtedly do so, with the aid of the disciples of Freud. There is no reason why the successful neutralization of nature cannot be extended to include human nature.

"Man has been clinging to the hope that has been his since he was delivered from feudalism—hope that he may live a life which is, in the words of Whitman, 'copious, vehement, spiritual, bold.' He is seeing that hope destroyed by instruments of his own devising, and the reverberations of his protest are shaking his earth.

"Perhaps this protest is only the last gasp of primitivism. Perhaps man feels that the traditions of his race demand of him a show of spirit before he submerges himself in the mass and that, when the little show is over, he will be glad enough to fall meekly into line. . . ."

Such were my unhappy thoughts in the winter of 1931–32, the winter of deepest depression and of the Lindbergh kidnapping. It was the year before Hitler came to power.

During the next two years I wrote five plays. Four of these went right into the bureau drawer, never to reappear. The fifth, "Acropolis," was produced in London and failed financially. It has never been done in the professional theatre in the United States. It was by all odds the best play I had written and the most positive affirmation of my own faith. It was a reaction, a rebellion against the despairing spirit of the "Reunion in Vienna" Preface, a rebellion that I have continued ever since. "Acropolis" was another historical analogy, but a legitimate one. The scene was Athens in the final years of the Periclean Age, when the triumph of Athenian democracy was being challenged by Spartan totalitarianism. It ended with some lines paraphrasing Pericles' funeral oration:

"I cannot give you any of the old words which say how fair and noble it is to die in battle. But I can give you the memory of our Commonwealth, as we have seen it and fallen in love with it, day by day. I can tell you, with truth, that the story of our Commonwealth will never die, but will live on, far away, woven into the fabric of other men's lives, in a world that is filled not with terror but with glory. . . ."

Some of these same words are in "There Shall Be No Night."

Following "Acropolis," I wrote "The Petrified

Forest." This was my first real attempt to write a play about my own country in my own time, to speak out directly. It contained its own Preface. In the following dialogue is the essence of this play:

SQUIER

I don't know anything. You see—the trouble with me is, I belong to a vanishing race. I'm one of the intellectuals.

GABBY

That means you've got brains. I can see you have.

SQUIER

Yes—brains without purpose. Noise without sound. Shape without substance. Have you ever read *The Hollow Men?*

(*She shakes her head.*)

Don't. It's discouraging, because it's true. It refers to the intellectuals, who thought they'd conquered Nature. They dammed it up, and used its waters to irrigate the wastelands. They built streamlined monstrosities to penetrate its resistance. They wrapped it up in cellophane and sold it in drugstores. They were so certain they had it subdued. And now—do you realize what it is that is causing world chaos?

GABBY

No.

SQUIER

Well, I'm probably the only living person who

can tell you. . . . It's Nature hitting back. Not
with the old weapons—floods, plagues, holocausts.
We can neutralize them. She's fighting back with
strange instruments called neuroses. She's delib-
erately afflicting mankind with the jitters. Nature
is proving that she can't be beaten—not by the
likes of us. She's taking the world away from the
intellectuals and giving it back to the apes . . .

Some of this is also in "There Shall Be No
Night."

"The Petrified Forest" was a negative, incon-
clusive sort of play, but I have a great fondness
for it because it pointed me in a new direction, and
that proved to be the way I really wanted to go.

"Idiot's Delight" was written in 1935. It was
about the outbreak of the second World War. It
was completely American in that it represented a
compound of blank pessimism and desperate optimism, of chaos and jazz. It was also representative of its author. I think I can say that completely typical of me was a speech spoken by
Harry Van, an itinerant, small-time showman. He
is conversing with a German bacteriologist, Doctor Waldersee, who is forced by war to end his
experiments on a cancer cure and devote himself
henceforth to the service of his country in dealing
out death. (The same problem as Doctor Valkonen's in "There Shall Be No Night.") Harry
Van tries to reassure this German victim of Naziism.

"I've remained an optimist," he says, "because I'm essentially a student of human nature. You dissect corpses and rats and similar unpleasant things. Well—it has been my job to dissect suckers! I've probed into the souls of some of the God-damnedest specimens. And what have I found? Now—don't sneer at me, Doctor—but above everything else I've found Faith! Faith in peace on earth, and good will to men—and faith that 'Muma,' the three-legged girl, really has got three legs. All my life, I've been selling phony goods to people of meagre intelligence and great faith. You'd think that would make me contemptuous of the human race, wouldn't you? But—on the contrary—it has given *me* Faith. It has made me sure that no matter how much the meek may be bulldozed or gypped—they *will* eventually inherit the earth."

"Idiot's Delight" was certainly an anti-war play; it was also violently anti-Fascist. In its postscript I wrote: "If people will continue to be intoxicated by the synthetic spirit of patriotism, pumped into them by megalomaniac leaders, and will continue to have faith in the 'security' provided by those lethal weapons sold to them by the armaments industry, then war is inevitable; and the world will soon resolve itself into the semblance of an ant hill, governed by commissars who owe their power to the profundity of their contempt for the individual members of their species." The point I was trying to make all through "Idiot's

Delight" is the same point that I have tried again to make in the radio speech by Doctor Valkonen in the first scene of "There Shall Be No Night."

Just half way between the writing of these two plays, in 1937, I wrote "Abe Lincoln in Illinois." That was a logical development, although I wasn't aware of it at the time. It was the story of a man of peace who had to face the issue of appeasement or war. He faced it. His "House Divided" speech made him a national figure and the candidate of the party which was determined to end slavery. Douglas accused Lincoln of "inflammatory persuasion," of "stimulating the passions of men to violence," but Lincoln did not retreat from the uncompromising stand which, after years of doubt and hesitancy, he had chosen to take. A few days after his inauguration as President, he was confronted with the grave situation of Fort Sumter. He asked his cabinet whether in their opinion he should send relief to Fort Sumter. The cabinet voted eight to one against doing so, on the ground that such action would most certainly mean war. Lincoln, on his own authority, ordered the relief to be sent to Fort Sumter. It did mean war—and for Lincoln it meant four years of anguish and then violent death. But it saved the Union.

The development of Lincoln's attitude in the years before the Civil War paralleled the development of the attitude of the whole American people in the years before 1940. Lincoln knew that slavery was an evil, but considered war a greater

evil. He served in Congress for one term during
the Mexican War, and in 1848 he denounced that
war, calling it a land grab, as indeed it was. His
"unpatriotic" stand at this time caused a newspaper in his own home state to denounce him as
"a second Benedict Arnold."

Lincoln then believed that, if the Southern
States wanted slavery, they were perfectly free to
have slavery. He didn't say much about this vital
issue; but when he talked at all, he expressed his
disapproval of the rabble-rousing agitations of
the Abolitionists. This was the liberal democratic
point of view of "live and let live." It was the
point of view of ordinary Americans—and Eng-
lishmen and Frenchmen, as well—in 1936 when
they said, "If the Germans want Naziism, or the
Italians Fascism, or the Russians Communism,
that is their business, and not ours." (I tried to
say in "Idiot's Delight" that it was everybody's
business. There is no more dangerous error of
foreign policy than for the government of one nation to say, "We are not concerned with the in-
ternal affairs of other nations.")

It was when Lincoln saw that the spirit of ac-
ceptance of slavery was spreading—from Missouri
into Kansas and Nebraska and on across the
plains and mountains to Oregon and California—
it was then that he turned from an appeaser into
a fighter.

While "Abe Lincoln in Illinois" was in rehearsal, in September, 1938, the Munich crisis

occurred. I showed Raymond Massey a passage from Lincoln's Peoria speech, of 1854, which seemed to have a direct bearing on the current situation. We decided to incorporate this into the speech which Mr. Massey delivered so brilliantly in the debate scene.

Lincoln, in this passage, was talking of the Douglas policy of "mind your own business"—the policy of indifference to evil—the policy of appeasement. He said he "could not but hate" it. "I hate it because of the monstrous injustice of slavery itself. I hate it because it deprives our republic of its just influence in the world; enables the enemies of free institutions everywhere to taunt us as hypocrites; causes the real friends of freedom to doubt our sincerity; and especially because it forces so many good men among ourselves into an open war with the very fundamentals of civil liberty, denying the good faith of the Declaration of Independence, and insisting that there is no right principle of action but *self-interest.*"

Those words have had a profound influence on my own thinking, or attempts at thought.

After "Abe Lincoln in Illinois," two years passed during which I had many doubts that I should ever write another play. I wanted to write about that which was uppermost in my own mind and in the minds of most other men who were still free to speak. But how could any play hope to compete or even keep up with the daily headlines

and the shrieks of increasing horror heard over
the radio? I said to my friend, Alexander Korda,
"I wish I could write a sparkling drawing-room
comedy without a suggestion of international calamity or social significance or anything else of
immediate importance." He laughed and said,
"Go ahead and write that comedy—and you'll find
that international calamity and social significance
are right there, in the drawing room."

With the outbreak of the second World War
in 1939 I was in a frenzy of uncertainty. I knew
all the arguments for keeping my own country
out of the European conflict; I had uttered many
of them myself, and at the top of my lungs. I had
learned that the forces which had got us into war
in 1917 were sympathy for the Allies and hatred
of German militarism, economic involvement with
the Allies, and the great national campaign for
preparedness which began at Plattsburg in 1915–
16. (I was there.) I believed that he that taketh
up the sword is going to use it, however he may
try to persuade himself, "I do this not because of
a desire to fight but because I wish to avoid fighting." That is why, for the twenty years which
followed 1918, I was a passionate advocate of
disarmament. It was a bitter moment for me when
I found myself on the same side as the Big Navy
enthusiasts.

All of these considerations were storming
around in my mind in September, 1939, and
storming with them was the conviction that Hit-

lerism was as great a menace to the United States as it was to any free country of Europe—that as a force it was far more formidable than most complacent people in the democracies supposed—that England and France, if we failed to help them, might crumble quickly before it and that then we should be helpless to oppose it.

Being myself so confused, I couldn't speak up with any positive conviction. I was terrified of identifying myself as a "Warmonger." But my mind was settled principally by two events: the first was a speech in October by Colonel Charles A. Lindbergh, which proved that Hitlerism was already powerfully and persuasively represented in our own midst; the second was the Soviet invasion of Finland.

Like many another who hopes that he is a Liberal, I had great faith in the Soviet Union as a force for world peace. I believed it was the mightiest opponent of Fascism. The Russian aid to the Spanish Loyalists and the Chinese substantiated that belief. Even after the news of the Nazi-Soviet treaty I continued to think wishfully that Stalin was playing his own shrewd game against Fascism. But with the assault on Finland the last scales of illusion fell. I knew that this was merely part of Hitler's game of world revolution; and it was not proletarian revolution—far from it; it was a new and immeasurably more virulent form of imperialism. The Soviet government was playing the old, inhuman game of power politics with

the same Machiavellian cynicism which has been
Fascism's deadliest weapon against the gullible
democracies. The Marxian principles of interna-
tionalism were as dead as Lenin. The Soviet war-
lords cared no more for the fate of the workers in
the United States than they had cared for the fate
of the workers in France. The sole purpose of
their propaganda in the United States, as it had
been in France, was to spread confusion and dis-
union, to weaken American resistance so that we
would provide an irresistible temptation to Hitler
to continue his conquests westward.

The reluctance of the United States to give help
to Finland shocked me. The sentiment of our people for the Finns was obvious. Here was a decent
little democracy, which had paid its debts and
played no part in any of the vicious European in-
trigues, ruthlessly assaulted by an overwhelm-
ingly superior force and gallantly fighting for its
own freedom. There could be only one reason for
America's reluctance to give any help to the
Finns, and that was abject fear. And if we were
in a state of abject fear, then we had already
been conquered by the masters of the Slave states
and we must surrender our birthright.

So I decided to raise my voice in protest against
the hysterical escapism, the Pontius Pilate retreat
from decision, which dominated American thinking and, despite all the warnings of the President
of the United States and the Secretary of State,
pointed our foreign policy toward suicidal isola-

tionism. I wrote this play in January and February, 1940, under constant pressure of the knowledge that it might at any moment be rendered hopelessly out of date. As it happened, the war in Finland ended while the play was in rehearsal. But the story of the Finns' three months of resistance continued to be the story of all decent, civilized people who choose to stand up and fight for their freedom against the forces of atavistic despotism. Shortly after the play's first opening, two more innocent countries, Denmark and Norway, were invaded by the Nazis. Then came the invasion and conquest of Holland, Belgium and France.

I was rather surprised, under the circumstances of writing, that this play developed a spirit of optimism along toward the end. But, in expressing my own essential faith, as I have tried to do herein, I couldn't very well keep optimism out. I believe every word that Doctor Valkonen utters in the sixth scene of "There Shall Be No Night." I believe that man, in his new-found consciousness, can find the means of his redemption. We are conscious of our past failures. We are conscious of our present perils. We must be conscious of our limitless future opportunities. We are armed with more bitter experience, more profound knowledge, than any generations that ever were in the history of the world. If we can't use this experience and this knowledge then the human story is really finished and we can go back and achieve forgetfulness and peace in the ooze from which we ascended.

It seems to me, as this Preface is written, that Doctor Valkonen's pessimism concerning man's mechanical defenses and his optimistic faith in man himself have been justified by events. The Mannerheim and Maginot Lines have gone. But the individual human spirit still lives and resists in the tortured streets of London.

I wish to express my gratitude to my family doctor, Charles Goodman Taylor, for the advice he gave me in forming the scientific philosophy of Doctor Valkonen; to W. L. White, for his broadcasts over C. B. S. from Finland—especially the deeply stirring one on Christmas Day, 1939—from which I gained almost all of my sketchy knowledge of the Soviet-Finnish War; to Anne Morrow Lindbergh, for an article of hers in the January, 1940, issue of the *Reader's Digest;* to my associates of the Playwrights' Company for invaluable suggestions for revisions in this hastily written play; and—for the third time in my life— to Lynn Fontanne and Alfred Lunt.

R. E. S.

September 13th, 1940

THERE SHALL BE NO NIGHT

SCENE I

The scene is the living room of the Valkonen house in the suburbs of Helsinki. It is afternoon of a day early in October, 1938.

This is a nice, neat, old-fashioned house, with large windows, through which one sees a lovely view of the harbor and the islands.

The room is comfortably furnished. On the walls, surprisingly, are pictures from an American house. The most prominent is a portrait of a handsome naval officer of the 1812 era. There are a dismal portrait of a substantial magnate of the 1880's, and a number of pallid little water-colors of Louisiana scenes. There is a charcoal drawing of a wistful looking gentleman. On the piano and on the tables are many photographs of famous doctors—Pavlov, Freud, the Mayos, Carrel, etc.

Up-stage, a large door leads into the dining room. An unseen door leads from this into the kitchen, to the right.

The main entrance, leading from the front hall, is lower right. The piano is upper left.

Near the center of the stage is a sofa, and in front of it, on a table, are a radio microphone and a telephone.

Wire connections for this equipment run out into

1

the dining room, where there are a mixer and other equipment.

Standing at the left of this table is Dr. Kaarlo Valkonen. *He is between forty-five and fifty years old—gentle, amused, vague, and now rather self-conscious. Beside him stands his wife,* Miranda, *who is beautiful, chic, and enjoying the whole situation intensely.* Kaarlo *is a native Finn;* Miranda *comes from New Bedford, Massachusetts.*

In the foreground are two Photographers *with flash cameras. They are taking pictures of the Valkonens.*

Toward the right stands Dave Corween, *an American, about thirty-five years old, formerly a newspaper foreign correspondent, now a European representative of the Columbia Broadcasting System.*

First Camera Man

Now—Doctor——

Kaarlo

Yes—I'm ready.

Miranda

Wait a minute——
(*She removes* Kaarlo's *glasses.*)

First Camera Man

Smile, please——
(*They both smile. The picture is taken. The* Camera Men *bow and cross to the left.*)

DAVE

Will you both sit down, please?

(KAARLO *and* MIRANDA *sit on the sofa.*)

Dr. Valkonen, would you look as though you were talking into the mike?

KAARLO

Talking?

MIRANDA

Just say something, Kaarlo—something thrilling and profound.

DAVE

Say 1–2–3–4–5–6–7—anything.

MIRANDA

And I'll look as if I were listening, fascinated.

DAVE (*smiles*)

That's right, Mrs. Valkonen.

FIRST CAMERA MAN

Ready?

(*They pose for an instant while he takes the picture. He changes negatives and takes several more pictures during* KAARLO's *speech.*)

DAVE

Can't you think of something? We want to test the microphone.

KAARLO (*nodding*)

Yes! I can think of something. (*He leans toward the microphone.*) How do you do, my dear friends in America? How are you? I am well. I hope you are likewise. And do you know that the human digestive tract or alimentary canal extends for a distance of twenty-five to thirty feet, and consists of the following main parts: the mouth, pharynx, œsophagus, stomach, small intestines, cæcum, large intestines, rectum and anus? Into this canal flow the secretions of the salivary glands, liver and pancreas. Don't I speak English nicely? Yes. Thank you. Is that enough?

(*The* CAMERA MEN *have finished and pack their equipment, preparing to leave.*)

DAVE

That was splendid, Doctor. Thank you very much.

SECOND CAMERA MAN

Thank you, Doctor.

KAARLO

Don't mention it, gentlemen.

MIRANDA

Will we get copies of those pictures?

FIRST CAMERA MAN

Oh yes, Mrs. Valkonen. We hope you will like them.

KAARLO

Thank you.

(*The* CAMERA MEN *bow and go out at the right.*)

DAVE (*calling toward the dining room*)
How was it, Gus?
(GUS *appears in the dining-room door. He is a young American radio mechanic.*)

GUS

It sounded fine. Just speak in that same natural way, Doctor.
(MIRANDA *turns to* DAVE *with some alarm.*)

MIRANDA

Was that radio on when he was talking?
(GUS *goes.*)

DAVE

Don't worry, Mrs. Valkonen. It was just a test. The voice went no farther than the next room.

MIRANDA

Now, Kaarlo—when you do speak to the American people, please don't forget yourself and go through all those disgusting organs again. People don't like to be reminded of such things.

KAARLO

But I don't know yet what I'm supposed to say. You haven't finished correcting that translation.

MIRANDA (*rising*)

I'll finish it now. Would you like a drink, Mr. Corween?

DAVE

Not just now, thank you.

MIRANDA

We'll all have a drink after the broadcast.

(*She goes out.* KAARLO *has been looking at the radio apparatus.*)

KAARLO

Wonderful business, this.

DAVE

Wonderful—and awful.

KAARLO

More complicated than the alimentary canal, eh?

DAVE

Perhaps. But less essential.

KAARLO

How does my voice get from here all the way to America? Can you explain that to me?

DAVE

No, Doctor—I can't. But I can give you the outline. The voice travels from the microphone along that wire into the next room. It goes into that box in there. That's called the mixer. From there, it goes over your own telephone line to the broadcasting station, where various things happen that I don't understand. It's then transmitted on another line under the Gulf of Finland to Geneva, where it's broadcast by short wave from the League of Nations station.

KAARLO

Really! So that's what the League of Nations is doing!

DAVE

Well, they've got to do something. They send your voice to some place on Long Island, where it's transmitted to C.B.S. in New York, and then re-broadcast from coast to coast.

KAARLO

My word! Do you think any one will listen?

DAVE (*laughing*)

Certainly. They'll listen to all sorts of strange things on Sunday.

KAARLO

I knew I should never have agreed to this non-sense. I'll make a fool of myself.

DAVE

Oh, please, Doctor—I didn't mean to suggest that——

KAARLO

I know you didn't. But I'm still sorry. My wife's relatives will be listening, and they will write to her and say, "Kaarlo sounds older." They live in New Bedford, Massachusetts. Have you ever been there?

DAVE

I couldn't be sure.

KAARLO

A depressing place. But good people. Terrifying—but good. All of these paintings on the wall came from the house in New Bedford. (*He points to the 1812 officer.*) There's a fine looking fellow. They must have been gayer in those days. But look at that one over there. Miranda's grandfather. Did you ever see such a brigand? That's a drawing of her father on the piano. A very sensitive face. He didn't come from New Bedford—Louisiana, I think. He painted all those water-colors—swamps, and things. Miranda loved him. He must have been very charming. But he was surely a very bad painter.

(UNCLE WALDEMAR *comes in from the right. He is a moody, disenchanted old man.* KAARLO *rises and crosses to him.*)

Ah, Uncle Waldemar—I was afraid you were going to be late. (KAARLO *kisses* UNCLE WALDEMAR.) This is Mr. Corween, of the American radio—my uncle Mr. Sederstrum.

DAVE

How do you do?

UNCLE WALDEMAR (*curtly*)

How do you do? (*He crosses to his easy chair at the left.*)

KAARLO

If you would like to have some music with the broadcast, Uncle Waldemar will play. A great musician. He plays the organ in the Agricola Church.

UNCLE WALDEMAR

Thank you. But I think you can do without music.

KAARLO

Look at this machine, Uncle Waldemar. (KAARLO *goes up to the couch and points to the microphone.*) My voice goes in there, and then into the dining room where it gets mixed, and then to the League of Nations, and then all over America. They will all be listening, because it's Sunday. (*He turns to* DAVE.) Will they hear me even in Minnesota?

DAVE

Yes, Doctor. Even in Minnesota.

KAARLO

It makes one frightened. (*He sits down.*)

DAVE

I know it does. I've been broadcasting for nearly a year now, all over Europe, and I still get mike fright when I hear that summons, "Come in, Vienna" or "Go ahead, Prague," or wherever I happen to be. (DAVE *sits down.*)

KAARLO

You were in Prague during the crisis?

DAVE

Yes—I just came from there—Prague and Munich.

KAARLO

You saw all of it, there in Munich?

DAVE

As much as we were allowed to see.

KAARLO

When we read our papers the day after that meeting last week—we just couldn't believe it. Something had happened that we couldn't understand. Could we, Uncle Waldemar?

UNCLE WALDEMAR

I could. I knew it would be a disaster.

KAARLO

Uncle Waldemar always looks on the dark side of things. There's been too much Sibelius in his life.

UNCLE WALDEMAR

I can understand what happened at Munich because I know Germany. I've lived there—I've studied music there—I've read Goethe. He knew his own people. He stood on the heights, and he said that from his point of view all life looks like some malignant disease.

DAVE

Well, he should see it now. I can tell you I was glad when they ordered me to come up here. You don't know what it means to be in a really free country again. To read newspapers that print *news*—to sit around cafes and hear people openly criticizing their government. Why—when I saw a girl in the street who wasn't afraid to use lipstick, I wanted to go right up and kiss her.

KAARLO

Why didn't you? She'd have been very flattered. Our girls here like Americans, especially those gay young college boys who come here on tours——

(MIRANDA *enters with the manuscript of the speech.* DAVE *and* KAARLO *rise.*)

MIRANDA

Here's your speech, Kaarlo. (*She gives him his speech and crosses to* UNCLE WALDEMAR, *kissing him.*) Hello, Uncle Waldemar. I'm sorry I missed church today, but there's been so much excitement around——

UNCLE WALDEMAR

It was just the same as always.

MIRANDA (*crossing back to the table*)

Kaarlo, you'd better read that speech all over to yourself first.

KAARLO

I'll go to our room and read it to the mirror. (*He goes out at the right.*)

DAVE

Dr. Valkonen showed me your family portraits.

MIRANDA

Oh, did he? Did he tell you his idea—that they represent the whole cycle of modern history? Rugged heroism—that's him—developing into ruthless materialism—that's him— (*She has pointed first to*

the 1812 ancestor, then the 1880 one. Then she crosses to the piano and picks up the drawing.)
—and then degenerating into intellectual impotence and decay—that's him. (*She holds the picture fondly.*) Rugged heroism—that's old great-grandfather Eustis—he fought in the navy in the war of 1812.

DAVE

Did he?

MIRANDA

Yes—and he lived to sail a clipper ship to California in the Gold Rush. He didn't get any gold, but he died happy. His son, my sainted grandfather—that's that one with the beard—bought his way out of the Civil War for three hundred dollars. Then he made a nice fortune selling shoddy uniforms to the army. He did even better after the war when he packed his carpet bag and went south. He married a beautiful daughter of the ruined aristocracy, and my father was the result. (*She holds out the drawing.*) You can see he was more New Orleans than New Bedford.

(DAVE *looks at the picture over her shoulder.*)
Sargent drew that. Fine drawing, isn't it?

DAVE

Superb.

MIRANDA (*crossing to the piano and replacing the drawing*)

Father avenged the honor of the Old South. When he came into possession of the family fortune, he went systematically to work and threw it away, squandered every penny that old whiskers there had scrounged and saved. And he had a wonderful time doing it. (*She gets a cigarette from a box on the piano and sits down.*) He was the idol of all the head waiters in London, Paris, Monte Carlo, Vienna. He took me along with him on his travels. He used to say to me, "Mandy, this won't last forever, but while it does, we're certainly going to make the most of it."

Dave

And how did you happen to meet Dr. Valkonen? (*He lights her cigarette.*)

Uncle Waldemar (*amused*)

Are you going to put all this on the radio?

Dave

Oh, no! But I'd like to write something about this visit. I try to maintain my status as a newspaper man against the day when the public will get tired of being fed through their ears.

Miranda

Well, Kaarlo and I met in Russia in 1914. That was when my father was coming to the end of his brilliant career as a spendthrift. Kaarlo was a medical officer in St. Petersburg—that's what they called it then. Oh, he was so handsome! Thin—

dark—tragic looking. I was seventeen—I'd never seen any one like him. Of course he didn't know I was alive. Then came the war and we had to leave for America. It was the end of the world for me. I pestered him with letters regularly, and he replied—once. After the revolution, he came to America to study, and we met again, and after considerable effort on my part, we were married. And that's all there is to that.

UNCLE WALDEMAR

Then he brought her back here, his American wife, and we asked him, "Is she rich?" and he said, "No." So we said, "Kaarlo is a fool."

MIRANDA

I've told you it wasn't his fault—he was too polite to refuse. (*She turns to* DAVE.) All that was a long time ago. I think Uncle Waldemar has forgiven me now.

DAVE

I hope I'll have the pleasure of meeting your son, Mrs. Valkonen.

MIRANDA

Oh, I hope so. We're expecting him any minute. He's been away on a holiday—working. They spend all their holidays in this country working. You've never seen such energetic people.

DAVE

I suppose your son is completely a Finn—not an American?

MIRANDA

He can't quite make up his mind what he is. But now he has his first girl friend. She'll probably settle the matter for him.

(KAARLO *comes in, carrying his speech.*)

KAARLO

Well, I've gone through this, and I must say it seems too dull, even for Sunday.

DAVE (*looking at his watch*)

It's pretty near time. I'll see if the connection is set.

(DAVE *goes into the dining room.* MIRANDA *rises and goes down to* UNCLE WALDEMAR. *She arranges the shawl on his lap.* KAARLO *paces up and down, reading his speech.*)

MIRANDA

How's the rheumatism, Uncle Waldemar?

UNCLE WALDEMAR

It's bad.

MIRANDA

Haven't those treatments done you any good?

UNCLE WALDEMAR

No.

MIRANDA

Never mind. We'll be going soon to Italy for a holiday and we'll take you. That will make you well.

(DAVE *returns and sits at the table, arranging his introductory speech.*)

UNCLE WALDEMAR

Yes—I know what those holidays are like, in Italy, or anywhere else. All Kaarlo does is visit lunatic asylums.

(DAVE *picks up the telephone, and looks toward* GUS *in the dining room.*)

GUS'S VOICE (*from the dining room*)

Go ahead.

DAVE (*into the telephone*)

Hello—hello. This is Dave Corween—Dave Corween. . . . Hello, Ed. How's everything? . . . Yes—I got here this morning. Beautiful place—lovely people—and what a relief. . . . Yes!! . . . No—I don't see how there can possibly be *another* crisis this year. . . . Maybe they'll let me come home for Christmas. . . . No—it's wonderfully quiet up here. Sweden, too. Yes—I came through Stockholm yesterday. (*To* KAARLO *and* MIRANDA.) If you'll sit down, we're about ready.

(*They sit on the sofa by the table.*)
How's the world series? . . . They did, eh. . . . Yes—I'm watching the time. 43½—O.K. (*He looks at his watch.*) . . . Good-bye, Ed.

MIRANDA (*to* KAARLO)

Good luck, darling—and just remember—it doesn't really matter.

Gus's Voice (*from the dining room*)

O.K., Dave.

DAVE

Listen!

VOICE FROM LOUD-SPEAKER

This is Station WABC in New York.

KAARLO

Great God!

MIRANDA

Did you hear that, Uncle Waldemar? It's New York!

UNCLE WALDEMAR

I heard.

(DAVE *cautions them to silence.*)

VOICE FROM LOUD-SPEAKER

We now take you to the Finnish capital. Go ahead, Helsinki.

(DAVE *speaks briskly into the microphone, using notes typed on copy paper.*)

DAVE

Hello America—this is David Corween, in Helsinki. We're bringing you the first of a series of broadcasts from Finland, Sweden and Norway, those little countries in the far north of Europe which are at peace, and intend to remain at peace. Finland is a country with a population about equal to that of Brooklyn. Like many other small nations, it achieved its freedom twenty years ago—but, unlike some of the others, it has consolidated

that freedom; it has made democracy work. It has
no minority problems. Its frontiers are disputed
by no one. Its people are rugged, honest, self-re-
specting and civilized.

(KAÀRLO *and* MIRANDA *start to speak to one
another.* DAVE *signals them to be quiet and goes
right on.*)

I am now speaking from the home of one of Finland's most distinguished citizens, Dr. Kaarlo
Valkonen, the eminent neurologist, who has received high honors in the United States, England,
the Soviet Union and other nations, and has just
been awarded the Nobel Prize in medicine. In
announcement of this award, the directors of the
Caroline Medical Institute in Stockholm stated
that Dr. Valkonen has given to mankind a new understanding of the true nature and the causes of
mental diseases—and I might add that those of us
who have to cover the European scene these days
can appreciate how much this understanding is
needed.

(KAARLO *is embarrassed and pained by all this;
he keeps looking at* MIRANDA, *who, however, is delighted.*)

Many of you have read his book, *The Defense of
Man,* and to some of you now listening he is known
personally, as he has lived much in America, and
his wife comes from that fine old Massachusetts
town, New Bedford. It gives me great pleasure to
bring you an outstanding servant of humanity—
Dr. Kaarlo Valkonen.

(*He moves the microphone over to* KAARLO *and gestures to him to begin.* MIRANDA *listens intently, waiting for mishaps.*)

KAARLO (*loudly*)

I never heard so much introduction.

(DAVE *moves the microphone back from* KAARLO *and signals him to speak more quietly.*)

To tell the truth, I think the Nobel prize is premature. The work I am doing will be finished by some one else many years from now. But still—I am glad to have that prize, as it enables us to go for a holiday in France and Italy, and my wife will buy some new clothes in Paris.

MIRANDA

Read what is written!

(KAARLO *looks for the first time at his manuscript.*)

KAARLO (*reading*)

Dr. Carrel has said, "For the first time in history, a crumbling civilization is capable of discerning the causes of its decay. For the first time it has at its disposal the gigantic strength of science." And he asks, "Will we utilize this knowledge and this power?" That's a question far more important than speculating about the possible results of the Munich crisis. In fact, behind this question are the real causes of all the problems we now must face.

It is no doubt well known to you that insanity is increasing at an alarming rate. Indeed, the day is within sight when the few remaining sane people are put into confinement and the lunatics are at large.

Does this seem a ridiculous exaggeration? Then look about you, at the present world. You see the spectacle of a great, brilliant nation, which has contributed perhaps more than all others to scientific progress. Today, the spiritual resistance of its people has been lowered to such an extent that they are willing to discard all their moral sense, all the essential principles of justice and civilization. They glorify a theory of government which is no more than co-ordinated barbarism, under the leadership of a megalomaniac who belongs in a psychopathic ward rather than a chancellery. He seeks to create a race of moral cretins whom science has rendered strong and germless in their bodies, but feeble and servile in their minds. We now know how quickly such men can be converted into brutes.

It is all very well to say, "We will go to war and crush this mighty force. Free men will always triumph over slaves." But after the war—and on into the centuries—what then? How long will these same free men possess the spiritual strength that enables them to be free? There is a problem for science to solve—and we must begin by admitting our own mistakes.

Science has considered disease as mechanical phenomena, to be cured by mechanical means. And we have been remarkably successful. Examine the achievements in the fight against tuberculosis—

typhoid—all the ancient plagues. You will see that the number of fatalities is steadily being reduced. Then look at the degenerative diseases—insanity, which is the degeneration of the brain—and cancer, which is degeneration of the tissues. These diseases are going up, almost in the same proportion as the others are going down.

Degeneration! That is the most terrifying word in the human vocabulary today. And doctors are beginning to ask, "Is there not a suspicious connection between our victories and our defeats? Are we perhaps saving children from measles and mumps that they may grow up to be neurotics and end their days in a mad-house?" Perhaps their early battles with disease toughen them. Perhaps without that essential experience, they go into maturity without having developed adequate defenses against life. What are these defenses?

St. Paul has said: "We glory in tribulation; knowing that tribulation worketh patience; and patience, experience; and experience, hope." We have been striving to eliminate tribulation, and as we have succeeded we have deprived man of his experience, and thus of his hope.

We have counted too heavily upon pills and serums to protect us from our enemies, just as we count too heavily upon vast systems of concrete fortifications and big navies to guard our frontiers. Of what avail are these artificial protections if each man lacks the power of resistance within himself?

I am not pleading for a return of measles and mumps. I am only saying that all of us have been trying too hard to find the easy way out—when man, to *be* man, needs the experience of the hard way. "There is no coming to consciousness without pain," in the words of Dr. Jung, and Science has provided no substitute for pain.

You have heard it said that the days of exploration are over—that there are no more lost continents—no more Eldorados. But I promise you that the greatest of all adventures in exploration is still before us—the exploration of man himself— his mind—his spirit—the thing we call his character —the quality which has raised him above the beasts.

"Know thyself," said the oracle. And after thousands of years, we still don't know. Can we learn before it is too late—before the process of man's degeneration has been completed and he is again a witless ape, groping his way back into the jungle? (*He looks up and thrusts his manuscript away.*) But why should I go on spoiling your Sunday? I want to send my greetings to New Bedford, Massachusetts. I want to send especial greetings to Minnesota, home of my dear good friends, the Mayos. Perhaps I have an especial feeling of love for Minnesota because it is so much like Finland, with many beautiful lakes, and forests of birch and pine and spruce. And I know so many fine people there, with good blood that came from Finland, and our neighboring countries of Sweden, Norway and Denmark.

To them, and to all my friends in the United States
of America I say, "Thank you and God bless you
and good-bye."

(*He turns to* MIRANDA *and shrugs as though to
say, "I'm sorry but that was the best I could do."*
MIRANDA *leans over and kisses him.*)

DAVE (*into the microphone*)
Thank you, Dr. Kaarlo Valkonen. This is David
Corween in Helsinki, returning you now to Colum-
bia in New York.

KAARLO	VOICE FROM LOUD-SPEAKER
Never will I speak to one of those damned things again.	We take you now to London. . . .

MIRANDA (*rising*)
Darling—you were wonderful! Didn't you think
it was fine, Uncle Waldemar?

UNCLE WALDEMAR
If they'll listen to that, they'll listen to anything.

DAVE (*rising*)
You were splendid, Doctor. A definite radio
personality.

MIRANDA
There!

KAARLO (*pleased*)
You really think so?

(GUS *comes in from the dining room to clear the
table of equipment.*)

MIRANDA

Of course he does. Now I'll go and mix the drinks. (*She goes off into the dining room.*)

GUS

They said it came through fine. I liked it myself. And I'm going to get that book of yours, Doctor. I probably can't understand it—but I'll bet it's good.

KAARLO

Why—thank you—thank you.

(GUS *goes out into the dining room.*)

What a charming man!

DAVE

I read your book last summer when I was resting between crises. And just the other day, when I heard I was coming up here about the Nobel Prize, I tried to get a copy in Munich. The bookseller assured me, solemnly, that there could be no such book, since he had never heard of it.

KAARLO (*rising*)

Of course, all my books are forbidden in Germany. I should be ashamed of myself if they weren't.

(ERIK VALKONEN *comes in from the right. He is seventeen years old, but mature and calm. He is handsome and healthy; there is a kind of quiet humor in his expression. With him is his girl friend,* KAATRI ALQUIST, *young, pretty, also healthy, and quite serious. Each of them carries a package.* KAARLO *goes immediately to* ERIK, *kisses him.*)

Erik! You're just too late for my broadcast. You missed something wonderful. Hello, Kaatri, my dear.

(KAATRI *curtsies to* KAARLO. ERIK *hands* KAARLO *his package.*)

ERIK

I brought you this from Viipuri, Father.

KAARLO

Viipurin Rinkelia! I'll have it with my coffee. (*He takes* KAATRI *over to* DAVE.) Let me introduce Miss Kaatri Alquist, Mr. Corween of the American radio. And my son, Erik.

(KAATRI *curtsies to* DAVE *and crosses to* UNCLE WALDEMAR. *After greeting her,* UNCLE WALDEMAR *points toward the dining room, as* ERIK *and* DAVE *shake hands.*)

ERIK AND DAVE

How do you do?

UNCLE WALDEMAR

Mrs. Valkonen is in the dining room.

(KAATRI *goes into the dining room.* ERIK *crosses to* UNCLE WALDEMAR.)

KAATRI'S VOICE

Hello, Mrs. Valkonen.

MIRANDA'S VOICE

Kaatri, how lovely!

ERIK (*kissing* UNCLE WALDEMAR)

Father says he was wonderful on the radio. Is that true?

UNCLE WALDEMAR

He only said the same things you've heard a hundred times before.

KAARLO

Erik, take this to your mother in the dining room.

(ERIK *takes the package from* KAARLO *and goes into the dining room.*)

ERIK

Mother! Mother! I'm back!

MIRANDA'S VOICE

Erik, darling! Did you have a good time?

KAARLO (*proudly*)

Fine boy, isn't he, Mr. Corween?

DAVE

Yes, fine. It's a shame he didn't hear your broadcast. He'd have been proud of you.

KAARLO

Oh—I'm an object of contempt to my own son—because, while I talk, he *acts*. He has been working on the Mannerheim Line.

DAVE

I'm afraid I don't know where that is.

KAARLO

It's on the isthmus—on the Russian frontier. It's our own little Maginot.

MIRANDA (*entering from the dining room with* ERIK *and* KAATRI)

Yes, he's a definite radio personality. . . . (*She puts the box of chocolates on the piano.*) Now we're going to have some coffee, and some Parker House Punch especially for you, Mr. Corween. Go and wash, children.

KAATRI

Yes, Mrs. Valkonen.

(*The two maids,* ILMA *and* LEMPI, *come in from the dining room with tablecloth, coffee urn, and service for six which they put on the table.*)

ERIK

You're not going just yet, Mr. Corween?

DAVE

Oh, no.

ERIK

Thank you. (*He bows and goes out after* KAATRI *at the right.*)

MIRANDA (*sitting on the sofa*)

You know, whenever any one comes home, from anywhere, there has to be a present. Kaatri brought me those chocolates, and Erik brought his father some of the bread they make in Viipuri. It's the custom of the country. Charming, isn't it?

DAVE

Yes. (*He starts to sit down.*)

MIRANDA (*under her breath*)

That's Uncle Waldemar's chair. Come and sit by me.

DAVE (*sitting on the couch*)

I've noticed that here—and in Sweden, too—everybody is insufferably polite. Why, yesterday, in Stockholm, my cab side-swiped another cab, so the two drivers got out and apologized to each other. It's unnatural.

(**UNCLE WALDEMAR** *sits at the coffee table.*)

MIRANDA

I know. I've lived here for twenty years. I've never got used to it. (*She is starting to pour the coffee.*)

KAARLO

I used to think, Mr. Corween, in my ignorance, that you Americans have no national character. My wife has taught me my error. Her character is strong enough to resist all civilizing influences. And sometimes I think our son has inherited too much from her. (*He sits down at the table.*)

MIRANDA

That's what Kaatri thinks. Kaatri is the girl friend I was telling you about. I'm afraid she disapproves of me. I'm too shallow—too frivolous.

KAARLO

Oh, Kaatri comes from a typically Finnish military family. Her father is a colonel and her brothers are all brought up to be fighters. Very formidable! Maybe she does disapprove of you, my dear, but in her heart she wishes she could be more like you. She wishes she could have as much fun as we do.

MIRANDA

I'll have a good talk with her some time.

DAVE

I'm interested in that work your son is doing.

KAARLO

I tell him it's silly—but he won't listen.

DAVE

It seems a sensible thing for any one to be preparing for trouble these days.

KAARLO

Yes—eminently sensible. But they don't know how to prepare. That's the trouble. They build those concrete pillboxes, and tank traps—as if such things could save anybody when Armageddon comes.

MIRANDA

What does it matter, darling? They enjoy doing the work.

KAARLO

Yes—and I suppose it's good exercise.

(ERIK *and* KAATRI *come in and go to chairs at the left, by the piano.*)
Erik and hundreds of other students spend all their free time on the Mannerheim Line. Kaatri is there, too, with the women's organization, to do the cooking and cleaning. Oh, they have a lot of fun—and maybe a little romance in the long evenings, eh, Kaatri?

KAATRI (*she giggles, then answers soberly*)

In the evening we have discussions, Dr. Valkonen.
(ERIK *brings* KAATRI *a cup of coffee.*)

DAVE

And may I ask—what sort of things do you discuss?

KAATRI

Last night we tried to arrive at some conclusions about the consequences of the Munich treaty.

DAVE

I'd like to know what your conclusions were?

ERIK

Just what you would probably hear in a similar discussion in America, Mr. Corween. We thanked heaven for the geography which puts us so far from the scene of action. We were grateful that we do not live in Czechoslovakia, or the Balkans, or even England or France.
(LEMPI *enters with the punch.*)

MIRANDA (*looking around*)

Ah—here it is! Here's the Parker House Punch, Mr. Corween. The old Parker House bar was the first place my father headed for after the reading of the will. I can't cook anything—but I can make the best rum punch and eggnog too. If you're ever here on New Year's Day, I'll give you some eggnog.

DAVE

I shall not forget that invitation. (*He is happy to be in the midst of such an untroubled, harmonious family.*)

ERIK

You came all the way here just to have my father broadcast?

KAARLO

You see?

DAVE

I'm ordered to travel around Scandinavia and pick up as many features as I can.

MIRANDA

I think we should drink a toast—to our benefactor, the late Alfred Nobel.
(*They all rise.*)

KAARLO

That's it—Nobel!

KAARLO AND MIRANDA

God bless him!

ERIK

The dynamite king.

MIRANDA

Hush, Erik. That's not in good taste.
(UNCLE WALDEMAR *crosses and sits at the piano. The others resume their seats.*)

KAARLO

As for me, I don't care where the money came from. Two million marks—forty thousand dollars.

MIRANDA (*reverting to New England*)
To say nothing of the solid gold medal.

KAARLO

To think I should see that much in a lifetime, let alone all at once.

DAVE (*to* ERIK)
What are you studying?

ERIK

Economics—sociology.

KAARLO

And ski-ing. He can't make up his mind whether he wants to be another Karl Marx, or another Olympic champion.

DAVE

Have you been much in the Soviet Union?

ERIK

Oh, yes. We lived there when father was working with Pavlov.

DAVE

And you really believe they might invade this country?

ERIK

If there were counter revolution in Russia, anything might happen. Or the Nazis might come that way. We have to be prepared.

MIRANDA

Erik, open the chocolates. Uncle Waldemar, play something. Play something gay. This is a celebration.

UNCLE WALDEMAR

I don't feel gay.

MIRANDA

Then drink this rum punch quickly and have a few more, and you'll forget your rheumatism. (*She takes him a glass of punch.*)

DAVE

Of course, the Nazis have been highly successful in terrifying people of the Bolshevik menace. But all the times I've been in Moscow, I've never seen anything but a passionate desire to be let alone, in peace.

(UNCLE WALDEMAR *starts to play a particularly gloomy selection by Sibelius.*)

KAARLO

Certainly. I know the Russians. I was a medical officer in their army and I was with them in

prison camp in Germany all through 1916. And
during the revolution I was right there in Leningrad on the staff of the Strelka Hospital. I treated
Lenin for a sore throat! And I can tell you about
these Russians: they love to plot—but they don't
love to fight. And the reason they don't love to
fight is that they're a little like the Italians—
they're too charming—they really don't know how
to hate.

(*During the foregoing speech the doorbell has
been heard, faintly, and* LEMPI *has crossed to the
right and gone out.*)

MIRANDA
Uncle Waldemar, what is that you're playing?

UNCLE WALDEMAR
Sibelius.

MIRANDA
Oh, darling, can't you play something a little
less solemn?

(LEMPI *returns and hands* MIRANDA *a card on a
silver plate.* UNCLE WALDEMAR *stops playing.*)
What is it? Oh, it's Dr. Ziemssen. Tell him to
come in.

(LEMPI *goes out.*)

KAARLO (*rising*)
Dr. Ziemssen is a neighbor of ours.

(DR. ZIEMSSEN *comes in. He is a mild, scholarly,
correct German of thirty-five or forty.* KAARLO
meets him at the door.)
Come in, Dr. Ziemssen. I'm delighted to see you.

ZEIMSSEN (*shaking* KAARLO's *hand*)

Herr Doktor.

(ZIEMSSEN *goes to* MIRANDA, *who rises and holds out her hand.* ZIEMSSEN *kisses it.*)

MIRANDA

How do you do, Dr. Ziemssen?

ZIEMSSEN

Frau Valkonen.

MIRANDA

You know Miss Alquist—and my family.

ZIEMSSEN (*bowing to each*)

Fräulein—Herr Sederstrum—Erik.

KAARLO

And may I introduce Mr. Corween of the American radio, Dr. Ziemssen.

ZIEMSSEN

Mr. Corween! I have heard a great deal of you.

DAVE (*sitting*)

Well—that's unusual.

KAARLO

Please——

(*Indicating a chair to* ZIEMSSEN.)

.Dr. Ziemssen is the German Consul General. He has heard of everybody. (KAARLO *sits down.*)

ZIEMSSEN (*smiles*)

Only the important people. I walked over, Herr Doktor, because I just this minute talked to Berlin on the telephone and they said they had heard your broadcast. They said it came through excellently and was highly entertaining.

DAVE

It was broadcast in Germany?

ZIEMSSEN

Oh, no. But it was heard at the government shortwave station.

KAARLO

Good God! I seem to remember that I said some things that were not for your government to hear.

ZIEMSSEN

Have no worries on that score, Herr Doktor. We are well accustomed to hearing the worst about ourselves. We have heard you frequently, Mr. Corween.

KAARLO

Don't be frightened by Dr. Ziemssen. He was an anthropologist before he became a diplomat. He is very broadminded.

MIRANDA

Will you have some American punch, Dr. Ziemssen?

ZIEMSSEN

Thank you, no.

KAARLO

Then have some coffee and I'll have another cup too—and some of that Viipurin rinkelia that Erik brought.

ZIEMSSEN

Viipurin Rinkelia! (*He turns to* ERIK.) Erik
—is the work getting on well?

ERIK

It seems to be. Of course I see only a small part
of it.

ZIEMSSEN

The Finnish defenses are magnificent. No one
will dare to challenge them.

ERIK

The Czechs had fine defenses, too.

ZIEMSSEN

Ah, but you are more intelligent than the Czechs.
You have no Allies—to betray you! (*He laughs at
that pleasantry.*) How do you feel about that,
Mr. Corween? You were at Munich.

DAVE

I'm afraid I have no feeling about anything.

MIRANDA

Then have some more punch, Mr. Corween.

DAVE (*laughs*)

No, thank you. (*To* ZIEMSSEN.) If you had
asked me that question a few years ago—if you had
asked me any questions of cosmic significance—I
could have answered without a moment's hesita-
tion. I was the youngest genius ever to be given a
by-line in *The Chicago Daily News*. I was on in-

timate terms with both God and Mammon. The
wisdom of the ages was set before me, on the half-
shell. All I had to do was add horseradish and eat.

ZIEMSSEN (*smiles*)

You have become a little less confident in recent
years?

DAVE

Well, since then I have been de-educated, if
there is such a word. I've covered Manchukuo,
Ethiopia, Spain, China, Austria, Czechoslovakia.
And all I can say is—I'm bewildered. But I suspect, Dr. Valkonen, that when you say the human
race is in danger of going insane, you're not so
much a prophet of future doom as a reporter of
current fact. (*He becomes conscious of the fact
that he is holding the floor. He smiles.*) I seem to
be sounding off. That punch is powerful.

MIRANDA

Good! Then have some more and tell us what
it was like in Ethiopia.

DAVE

Thank you. I mustn't. I must try to find out
what it's like here. (*To* ERIK.) Do you suppose I
could get permission to visit those defenses you're
working on?

ERIK

I should think so. Planes from Leningrad are
flying over that region all the time, so I don't believe there's much secrecy.

DAVE

I must try to get there. There might be material for a broadcast.

KAARLO

If there's anything I can do—any letters of introduction?

DAVE (*rising*)

Oh, no, thank you. I'm trained to push in anywhere. Thank you very much, Mrs. Valkonen. You've been very kind. . . .

MIRANDA (*shaking hands with him*)

And you've been very nice. I hope you'll come and see us again.

DAVE

I'll probably be back some time. (*He crosses to shake hands with* ERIK.) Certainly in 1940 for the Olympic games. Good-bye, Mr. Valkonen.

ERIK

Good-bye, Mr. Corween.

DAVE (*to each in turn*)

Good-bye, Miss Alquist. (*To* UNCLE WALDEMAR.) Good-bye, sir—please don't get up. (*To* ZIEMSSEN.) Good-bye, sir. (*He crosses to* KAARLO.) Good-bye, Doctor——

KAARLO

Oh, I'll see you to the door.

(*They go out at the right.* MIRANDA, KAATRI, *and* ZIEMSSEN *sit.*)

MIRANDA

Do you like him, Erik? He's nice, isn't he?

ERIK

Yes. I wish I could do work like that. To be able to wander all over the earth—and see things—without being a part of them.

(KAATRI *darts a worried look at* ERIK. *She knows he is now talking with his mother's voice.*)

KAATRI (*with surprising vehemence*)

I'd hate such a life!

MIRANDA

Why, Kaatri?

KAATRI

When you see too much of the world it makes you cynical. I'd never want to be that.

MIRANDA

I shouldn't either. But I've travelled all over and it hasn't made me cynical. Perhaps that's because I'm just plain stupid.

ZIEMSSEN

Ah no, Frau Valkonen. It is only because you are an American.

ERIK

A journalist like Mr. Corween has the opportunity to see the *truth*. Maybe the ultimate truth is the ultimate futility——

MIRANDA (*laughing at this*)

Oh, dear. That boy really should have a beard.

ERIK

Even so—I'd like to know the truth about the world. All of it!

(UNCLE WALDEMAR *starts to play a gay tune.*)

MIRANDA

Kaatri, the next time we go to America, I'll ask your father and mother if you can go with us. Would you like that?

KAATRI

Oh, I think I should love that!

(KAARLO *returns and sits beside* MIRANDA.)

KAARLO

I hope some of your relatives will send us a cable so we'll know how I really sounded.

MIRANDA (*again reverting to New England*)

If I know New Bedford, they'll send a postcard. . . . What's that you're playing now, Uncle Waldemar?

(UNCLE WALDEMAR *doesn't hear. She turns to* DR. ZIEMSSEN.)
What is that?

ZIEMSSEN (*listening, appreciatively*)

I believe that is Merikantor's "Tolari Ja Huotari," isn't it? (*He listens for a moment.*) Yes— a delightful little Finnish folk song.

(UNCLE WALDEMAR *continues to play, with tinkling variations on the theme.*)

MIRANDA

Oh—I love that.

(*She pats* KAARLO's *hand. They listen silently, happily to the music.*)

CURTAIN

SCENE II

The same. An evening late in November, 1939.

KAATRI *is sitting on the couch, looking toward* ERIK, *who is at the window by the piano, looking out.* KAATRI *is crocheting.*

KAATRI

What are you looking at, Erik?

ERIK (*who obviously has to think for an instant before answering this question*)

I'm looking at the stars.

KAATRI

Oh.

ERIK

There are millions of them. They're so bright you can see them reflected on the snow.

KAATRI

I know why you're looking out the window, Erik. Many people are looking out of their windows to-night—watching for the bombers.

ERIK (*turning from the window*)

Now, Kaatri! There are no bombers coming here.

KAATRI

That's what they said in Poland. I'm sure they kept telling themselves, "The bombers won't come.

43

Something will happen. There'll be another Munich. There'll be a revloution in Germany. The United States will forbid Europe to have a war. *Something* is sure to happen to prevent the bombers from coming to Poland." But they did come.

ERIK

They were Nazis.

KAATRI

The Russians went into Poland, too.

ERIK

Yes, and why not? The Nazis had done the work. (*He comes over and sits near her.*) All the Russians had to do was march in and take all that territory at no cost to themselves. But—they know perfectly well if they attack us it would mean betrayal of the revolution! The suffering they might inflict on us would be insignificant compared to the murder of their own honor.

KAATRI

Honor!

ERIK

That's what my father says, and he knows them.

KAATRI (*putting down her crocheting*)

I don't believe they ever had any honor—Tsarists or Bolshevists either. My father knows them, too. That's why he has spent his life preparing to fight them when they invade our country.

ERIK (*laughs*)

Oh—Kaatri—don't let's sit here telling each other what our fathers say. We're old enough to make up our own minds, aren't we?

KAATRI

I don't know, Erik.

ERIK

You've made up your mind that we're going to be married, haven't you?

KAATRI

Yes. (*She laughs, shyly.*) But—that's different.

ERIK

I'm glad it *is* different. The trouble with old people is—they remember too much—old wars, old hates. They can't get those things out of their minds. But we have no such memories. We're free of such ugly things. If there's going to be a better future, we're the ones who are going to make it. (*He takes her hands.*) Kaatri——

KAATRI

Yes, Erik?

ERIK

Next summer I'll stop being a student. I'll be a worker! And you and I will be married.

KAATRI (*thrilled*)

What will we live on, Erik?

ERIK (*heroically*)

On what I make. It won't be much—but it will be enough. I'll be your man—and you'll be my woman.

(*They both draw apart, laugh, and then they kiss.*)

KAATRI

We'll have a wonderful wedding, won't we, Erik?

ERIK

Yes—I suppose our families will insist on that. (*They are still in each other's arms.*)

KAATRI

It will be in the Agricola Church, and there'll be lots of flowers.

ERIK

Your father will be looking stern and magnificent in his colonel's uniform. And my father, in his black coat, looking bored. And Mother behaving like a grand duchess, and Uncle Waldemar playing da-da-de-dum. . . . (*He hums a bar of the Wedding March.*) And then we'll escape from all of them, and go home, and have several children.

KAATRI

Erik!

(*They both laugh happily and kiss each other again.*)

ERIK

Oh, Kaatri! We'll be happy people, you and I. That's all that matters, isn't it, dearest?

KAATRI

Yes. (*Suddenly the happiness fades from her face.*) No! It isn't all that matters!

ERIK

What else is there?

KAATRI (*looking away from him, but still holding him close*)

There's *now.* . . . There's this. . . . There may be war. Next summer may never come to us.

ERIK

I tell you—we don't have to think about those things. We're young, and we're free. We have only our own love, for each other.

(UNCLE WALDEMAR *comes in. He carries a newspaper. He looks at them. They break apart guiltily, rise, and confront him with great embarrassment.*)

Oh, please forgive me, Uncle Waldemar. We were——

UNCLE WALDEMAR

Yes.

ERIK

We were only——

UNCLE WALDEMAR

I saw what you were doing. I'm sorry to have interrupted. (*He kisses* KAATRI, *then* ERIK, *and crosses to the piano.* KAATRI *sits down again.*) But there's some news here.

ERIK

What is it?

UNCLE WALDEMAR

It may be good. Our government has received a message from the United States government, from Washington. They also sent the same message to Moscow. (*He comes close to them.*) It's offering their good offices to settle the Soviet-Finnish dispute. That's what they call it—the dispute. Here's what they say.

(*As he starts to read,* ERIK *sits on the sofa beside* KAATRI.)

"We would view with extreme regret any extension of the present area of war and the consequent further deterioration of international relations." That's what they say in Washington.

KAATRI (*who is holding* ERIK'*s hand*)

Do you suppose the Russians will listen to that?

ERIK

Of course they'll listen.

KAATRI

Erik believes they won't attack us. What do you believe, Uncle Waldemar?

UNCLE WALDEMAR

I know they *will!*

KAATRI (*to* ERIK)

There!

UNCLE WALDEMAR

Do you know what the press in Moscow is saying about us? We're "that Finnish scum"—we're "bourgeois bandits"—"Tools of British imperialism"—"Fascist assassins." (*He crosses to the left and flings the newspaper onto the piano.*) Those words are the advance guard of the Red Army!

ERIK

My father doesn't agree with you.

UNCLE WALDEMAR

And what does *he* know about it?

ERIK

As much as any one could. He understands the Russians. He was the good friend of Pavlov and Gorki, and even Lenin himself.

UNCLE WALDEMAR

All those gentlemen you mention are dead. And the revolution—that's dead, too. It's embalmed and exposed in a glass coffin in front of the Kremlin. It is respected—but dead. Now comes the true disintegration—the end of the world. Your father said—men might become again like apes, groping their way back into the jungle. Well—it has come to pass. Men are groping their way through the night. The lights are out in Berlin, Paris, London. And in Warsaw, they crawl through the ruins like rats. It will be the same here. This is war in the jungle, and the winner will be crowned "King of Beasts."

(MIRANDA *comes in from the right, looking very smart in her furs and her Paris hat.* ERIK *and* KAATRI *rise.*)

ERIK

Hello, Mother. Where's Father?

MIRANDA (*taking off her hat and coat*)

He's at the laboratory. (*She puts her wraps on a chair at the right.*) I went there to try to make him come home. He had a lot of dogs there—there must have been thirty or forty of them—all barking and howling. I asked him what he was doing with all those dogs, but he told me to go away. (*She kisses* KAATRI.) Kaatri—are your mother and father well?

KAATRI

My mother is well, thank you. My father is with the army in the north.

MIRANDA

But he'll surely be home for Christmas?

KAATRI

Oh, yes, Mrs. Valkonen—we hope so.

(MIRANDA *has come up to* ERIK. *She kisses him.*)

UNCLE WALDEMAR

I have to go to the church and practice. There's to be a great service this evening—prayers for peace.

MIRANDA (*sitting down on the sofa*)

I know.

UNCLE WALDEMAR

The President will be there and the Cabinet and the leaders of all parties. (*He starts to cross toward the door at the right.*) Tonight—prayers. Tomorrow—guns. (*He goes out. There is a moment of constrained silence.*)

MIRANDA

I stopped in at the American Legation on my way home and saw Mr. Walsh. I wanted to find out if he had any news. He told me that the State Department has ordered all Americans to leave Finland at once. He was very guarded in his choice of words—but he seems to think that things are rather serious.

ERIK

So does Uncle Waldemar. But that doesn't mean anything. The American government—all governments—are being pulverized with fear by this Soviet propaganda. (*He picks up the paper from the piano.*) They want to pulverize us, too, so that we'll give them what they want without a struggle. It's all bluff—it's all an imitation of the Nazis.

KAATRI

But when the bluff doesn't work, suppose they go on imitating the Nazis—suppose they do attack?

(MIRANDA *looks from* KAATRI *to* ERIK, *awaiting his reply.*)

ERIK (*without emotion*)

Then—we'll have to fight—that's all.

MIRANDA

But—how can we fight?

ERIK

To the best of our ability.

MIRANDA

And how long will that last?

ERIK

A few days—a few weeks—I don't know. (*He is looking out the window.*)

MIRANDA

Erik—*Erik!*
(*He turns to her.*)
Would *you* fight?

ERIK

Of course I would. Everybody would!

MIRANDA

Why? What good would that do?

ERIK

It would prove that this country has a right to live.

MIRANDA

And who will derive any benefit from that proof? Are you anxious to die just to get applause from the civilized world—applause and probably nothing else? The Czechs are fine, brave people—but they didn't offer any resistance to the Germans.

ERIK

They couldn't. Their resistance was stolen from them at Munich.

MIRANDA

Even so—they're better off now than the Poles, who did resist.

ERIK

That doesn't affect my feeling. I only know that if any one is going to take my freedom from me, he's going to have to pay for it.

MIRANDA

Now you're talking like a boy scout.

ERIK

I'm your son, Mother. I have the same blood in me that you have—the blood of that gentleman up there. (*He points to the portrait of great-grandfather Eustis.*) He fought pirates in the Mediterranean. He fought with Jackson at New Orleans.

MIRANDA

Yes—and when he died, in honored old age, they had to pass the hat around among the neighbors to get enough to bury him. . . . (*Pointing to the portrait of her grandfather.*) Whereas that unselfish hero who paid another man to take his place in the conscript army—when he died—the whole town turned out—the Chamber of Commerce, the Republican Club, the Knights of Pythias—all paying tribute to the memory of a good, substantial citizen. If you have to look to your ancestry for guidance, look to him. He was no hero. He was a despicable, slimy cheat. But he did very well. . . . You say some one will have to pay for your freedom. But who will receive the payment? Not you, when you're dead.

KAATRI (fiercely)

Don't listen to her, Erik! Don't listen to her!

MIRANDA (amiably)

Why shouldn't he listen to me, Kaatri?

KAATRI (with too much vehemence)

Because you're an American! You don't understand.

MIRANDA (patiently)

I understand one thing, Kaatri. Erik is my son. I want to save his life.

KAATRI

What good is his life if it has to be spent in slavery? (To ERIK.) And that's what it would be if he gave in to them. Slavery for you—for all of us. Oh, I know that you Americans don't like to think of such terrible things.

ERIK

Kaatri! You mustn't say that——

MIRANDA (*gently*)

You may say what you please about me, Kaatri.
But you can't say it about Erik. He's as loyal as
you are. He was born in this house, as his father
was before him.

KAATRI

Dr. Valkonen is like you. He doesn't really belong to this country. He is a great scientist. He
has an international mind.

MIRANDA

And is that a bad thing?

KAATRI

Oh, no—it's a good thing—a noble thing. But
for Erik—it would be weakness. I'm afraid for
Erik—afraid that he belongs more to America than
he does to us. Oh—I don't want to be rude, Mrs.
Valkonen—to you or your country. But we're desperate people now. All the men in my family—my
father, my brothers—they're all in the army now,
on the frontier. It's the same with all families,
rich and poor, men and women. All our lives we've
had to be ready to fight, for everything we are,
everything we believe in. Oh, I know—it's hard for
you to understand that—or to see the *need* for it
that is in our souls.

ERIK

Kaatri! Of course Mother can understand!
Americans fought for that same thing—for the
same reason—the same need, that was in their souls.

It was Americans who taught the whole world that it was *worth* fighting for!

KAATRI

Yes. But—it's just as Dr. Valkonen says. When life becomes too easy for people, something changes in their character, something is lost. Americans now are too lucky. (*She looks straight at* MIRANDA.) In your blood is the water of those oceans that have made your country safe. But—don't try to persuade Erik that life here is as easy as it is in America. (*She is speaking passionately, desperately.*) He's a Finn, and the time has come when he must behave like one.

ERIK

Kaatri—my dearest— (*Crossing behind the sofa, he puts a hand on* KAATRI's *right shoulder. She buries her head against him.*) Don't—don't cry.

(*The word "dearest" makes an emphatic impression on* MIRANDA. *She stares at them.*)

MIRANDA

Kaatri—Kaatri—are you and Erik really in love with each other?

ERIK

Mother!

MIRANDA

Darling, I started to talk to you as though you were still a child—and I wanted first to reason with you—and then if that failed, I would *forbid* you to throw your life away for a lost cause. And then

Kaatri spoke up, and you called her "dearest," and that one word stopped me short. I asked Kaatri that question because I thought the answer might help me to understand this strange, new fact—that you're not my son any more. You're a man. . . . Of course, you don't have to answer.

ERIK (*his hand on* KAATRI'S *shoulder*)
We do love each other. We are going to be married.

MIRANDA (*after a pause, kisses* KAATRI)
Erik—Kaatri—I'm glad! I'm glad.

KAARLO'S VOICE (*from off-stage, right*)
Erik!
(ERIK *goes to the door.*)
Erik! You know those litters of puppies that I separated—eight litters?

ERIK
Yes, Father.

KAARLO (*entering, he throws an arm across* ERIK'S *shoulders and leads him as he talks*)
The dogs have just come back from Rovaniemi— the ones I sent up there last year. The most wonderful results. I've tested them in every way. Out of thirty-one dogs, seven are definitely——

MIRANDA (*breaking in*)
Kaarlo! Kaarlo!

KAARLO

Yes, my dear. (*He slips out of his coat. To* ERIK.) Take this. (*To* MIRANDA.) I want to apologize for being a little bit irritable when you came into the laboratory—but I was excited. Those dogs. . . .

MIRANDA

Never mind about that. I have something to tell you.

(*She looks questioningly from* KAATRI *to* ERIK, *who nod permission for her to speak.*)

KAARLO (*waiting, sits*)

Yes? . . . Well?

MIRANDA

Erik and Kaatri are going to be married.

KAARLO

Erik? (*He looks at him, wonderingly, and then bursts out laughing.*)

MIRANDA (*reproachfully*)

Kaarlo!

KAARLO (*still laughing*)

Forgive me—but——

MIRANDA

Don't laugh. Now, it's not funny, Kaarlo.

KAARLO

No. No.

MIRANDA

No.

KAARLO

No, I know it isn't.

MIRANDA

Darling—you should congratulate them at least.

ERIK

Oh, let him laugh, Mother. Perhaps it *is* funny.

KAARLO

No, no. (*Rises.*) I *do* congratulate you, Erik.
And as for you, Kaatri—
(*She rises as he goes to her*)
—you're a sweet girl and I shall be delighted to
have you for a daughter-in-law. (*He kisses her.*)

KAATRI (*curtsying*)

Thank you, Dr. Valkonen.

KAARLO

Ever since Erik was born I've been training him
to be a gentleman of taste and discrimination, and,
by God, I've succeeded. (*To* ERIK.) Again I congratulate you and thank you for justifying me.
It's really—it's unbelievable. *You*—a bridegroom!
(*He kisses him.*) But we must have some schnapps
—a toast to the happy couple. And then we will
all have supper.

MIRANDA

Oh darling, we're having supper later, tonight.
I told the maids they could go to church. And

we're all going to church, too. Come with us, Kaarlo. You must go and put on your tail coat.

KAARLO

And why must we all go to church?

MIRANDA

Oh, there's going to be a great service. The President and everybody will be there. We're going to pray that this country will be able to defend itself.

(KAARLO's *amusement fades instantly.*)

KAARLO

Oh! So that's it! All day I have had the utmost difficulty persuading my assistants to attend to their duties. All they wanted to think about and talk about was would we or would we not have to fight the Soviet Union? I don't want to hear any of that talk here.

MIRANDA

Neither do I, Kaarlo. But I've had to hear it. Erik is ready to fight.

KAARLO

Erik? (*He turns coldly to* ERIK.) You're a child. It seems to me that you are deciding too suddenly that you are grown up. If you want to consider yourself engaged to be married, I have no objection—I'm delighted. But I don't want to hear that you are talking to your mother, or to any one else, about going to war.

ERIK

I'm sorry, father—but I have to do what I think best.

KAARLO

And are you *able* to think?

MIRANDA

Oh, Kaarlo! Of course Erik knows——

KAARLO

No, Miranda. Don't interrupt. (*To* ERIK.) I repeat—in forming this heroic resolve to fight— have you used one grain of the intelligence that I know you possess?

ERIK

I hope I have.

KAARLO

Hoping is not good enough. You have seen those celebrations in Red Square—all those aero-planes, those huge tanks, those troops marching— hundreds of thousands of them?

ERIK

Yes, Father—I've seen them.

KAARLO

And yet you dare to pretend you're competent to stand up against such a force as that?

ERIK

That's why I've trained with the volunteer ski troops—and why I've worked to help make the

Mannerheim Line so strong they can never break
through.

KAARLO

All that nonsensical child's play on skis——

ERIK

Kaatri's brother Vaino is younger than I am—
but he's with his father's regiment at the frontier . . .

KAARLO (*bitterly*)

Oh! If we are at war with the Soviet Union, *I*
shall be at the frontier, too. Surely we'll need
everybody, including the aged and decrepit.

MIRANDA

Now, really, Kaarlo, that is just simply ridiculous——

KAARLO (*sitting*)

I can press the trigger of a machine gun just
as well as Erik. . . . So that's what we're going to
pray for? Ability to imitate our enemies in the
display of force. It is all nothing but a substitute
for intelligent thinking.

ERIK

This is not a time for intelligent thinking! That
doesn't do any good.

KAARLO

No?

ERIK

When your enemies are relying on force, you
can't meet them with theories. You can't throw

books at them—even good books. What else can anybody do but fight?

KAARLO (*bitterly*)

This is no time for intelligent thinking! So this is the climax of a century of scientific miracles. This is what the great men worked for—what *they* fought for in their laboratories. Pasteur, Koch, Ehrlich, Lister. They saved lives that we might build Mannerheim Lines in which to die.

(*Church bells are heard faintly in the distance.*)

MIRANDA

Now—that's enough, Kaarlo. (*Rising.*) If you don't want to go to church, you don't have to. We'll go by ourselves.

KAARLO (*rising*)

Oh, I'll put on my tail coat and go with you. I'll join in asking God to grant the impossible. But I reserve the right to say my own prayers.

(*He goes out.* MIRANDA, *who has been putting on her hat and coat, crosses to* ERIK.)

MIRANDA

We'll be ready in a few minutes. And, Erik— you must not say any more to your father about going to war.

ERIK

I'll try not to, Mother.

(MIRANDA *goes out.*)

Poor father! This is a terrible thing for him—for

a man of great faith, as he is. The rest of us
have nothing to lose but our lives.

(KAATRI *goes to* ERIK—*takes hold of him.*)

KAATRI

Erik—I love you—I do love you, and I'm sorry I
said things tonight that only made you more unhappy. I wasn't much help to you.

ERIK (*holding her tightly*)

All you said was true, Kaatri. I'm glad you
said it. I have to see things clearly. I have to see
my mother and father as they are. They don't
really live in this country—in this time. They live
together in the future—the future as my father
has imagined it—not the one that may be made by
unimaginative men. They are wonderful people—
both of them—wonderful and unreal. You *are*
real. You know what we have to face—and we will
face it without fear.

(*He kisses her, passionately.*)

KAARLO (*entering*)

This coat reeks of moth balls. It will be a
scandal in church.

MIRANDA (*offstage*)

Don't worry, Kaarlo. There'll be so much of
that smell in church they won't even notice you.
Have you a clean handkerchief?

KAARLO

Will you bring me one, please?

(ERIK *helps* KAARLO *with his coat.*)

Get your coat on, Kaatri, my dear—and you too, Erik.

ERIK

Yes, father.

(ERIK *and* KAATRI *go out.* MIRANDA *enters, and puts a handkerchief into* KAARLO'S *coat pocket. He kisses her cheek.*)

KAARLO

Come, Miranda—we go to pray.

(*They start out toward the right.*)

O God, have pity, for that which we have greatly feared has come upon us.

(*He switches off the lights. The room is in darkness, except for the moonlight from the windows. The church bells can still be heard.*)

CURTAIN

SCENE III

The same. Next afternoon.

UNCLE WALDEMAR *comes in from the right, and is surprised to see black drapes at all the windows. They are now drawn apart to let the sun in. He inspects them, goes to the piano, sits, starts to play.*

MIRANDA *calls from the dining room.*

MIRANDA'S VOICE

Uncle Waldemar!

UNCLE WALDEMAR

Yes?

MIRANDA'S VOICE

Are Kaarlo and Erik with you?

UNCLE WALDEMAR

No.

(MIRANDA *comes in from the dining room. She is wearing an apron and carrying a dust cloth.*)

MIRANDA

Have you seen them?

UNCLE WALDEMAR

I saw Kaarlo. I stopped at the hospital.

MIRANDA

Is he all right?

66

UNCLE WALDEMAR

Yes.

(*Greatly relieved, she kisses him.*)

MIRANDA

And Erik?

UNCLE WALDEMAR

Oh, I don't know anything about him. I thought he was here.

MIRANDA

I haven't seen him since the church service last night. He took Kaatri home and got in very late and then he was off this morning even before I was up.

UNCLE WALDEMAR

Probably he's with Kaatri now, at the Alquists' house.

MIRANDA

Did any bombs fall in that part of the city?

UNCLE WALDEMAR

No. I passed there on my way home. There was no damage there.

MIRANDA

Was the air raid bad?

UNCLE WALDEMAR

Not nearly as bad as expected. Maybe about thirty people killed.

MIRANDA

That's what the policeman told me.

UNCLE WALDEMAR

Were the police here?

MIRANDA

Yes, I was ordered to put up those black curtains on the windows before nightfall. There must be no light from the windows. . . . Oh, I'm so glad to see you, Uncle Waldemar. I've been alone here all day . . .

UNCLE WALDEMAR

Alone? Where are Ilma and Lempi?

MIRANDA

They're gone. They're both in the Lottas. From now on all of us will have to eat my cooking. It's three o'clock in the afternoon, and I just finished making the beds. They look frightful. . . . I wish Kaarlo and Erik would come home! What was Kaarlo doing at the hospital?

UNCLE WALDEMAR

I don't know. I saw him only for a moment. He had a white coat on.

(MIRANDA *starts dusting the furniture.*)

MIRANDA

When he left here this morning for the hospital, he said it was a good joke—his trying to be a doctor again—when it's been fifteen years since he even gave anybody an aspirin tablet.

Uncle Waldemar (*coming down from the piano*)
Miranda——

MIRANDA

Yes, Uncle Waldemar.
(*She is kneeling, dusting.*)

Uncle Waldemar (*with apparent difficulty*)

Miranda, I want to tell you that I am sorry for
many things that I have said.

MIRANDA

What things?

Uncle Waldemar

I've talked too much about the troubles of the
world.

MIRANDA

And why should you feel you have to apologize
for that?

Uncle Waldemar

Because now I am deeply distressed.

MIRANDA

I know you are. We're all distressed. But
there's nothing we can do about it.

Uncle Waldemar

I have been a poor companion for you and
Kaarlo. It wasn't so bad for Kaarlo because he
paid no attention. But you have been so good and
kind—to me and all of us here. You came here a
stranger, and you made all of us love you.

MIRANDA (*harshly*)

Now, for God's sake, Uncle Waldemar, don't let's have any of that!

UNCLE WALDEMAR

But there are things on my mind, and I want to say them. You have worked so hard and so well to make this a happy home——

MIRANDA (*dusting the sofa*)

I've never done any work in my life, and I've never wanted to.

UNCLE WALDEMAR

But you have filled this house with laughter— your own peculiar American kind of laughter. And here I have been, in the midst of all this happiness, an apostle of despair.

MIRANDA

And so you want to be forgiven for telling the truth?

UNCLE WALDEMAR (*with bitter self-accusation*)

I should have had more philosophy! I—who lived for forty years under the tyranny of the Tsars— and then saw my country rise up from the ashes of the war and the revolution. I should have been reconciled to this. And you—you never saw anything of such real misery in your country. But now—when this came—you took it calmly. You showed wisdom.

MIRANDA

I took it calmly because I didn't know what was coming. I never believed it could happen. I don't believe it now. Look at me, dusting the furniture in the face of the enemy! Did you ever see such a confession of utter helplessness? (*She tosses the dust-rag aside and sits down on the sofa.*)

UNCLE WALDEMAR

You like to believe you are merely frivolous. But you're not so foreign to us solemn Finns as you think. You're a daughter of the Puritans, who would resist any oppression, undergo any sacrifice, in order to worship God in their own way. . . . I have always believed in God's mercy. I have served Him in His church. Whenever I was in doubt and fear, I would go back to the teachings of Martin Luther—to the doctrine of "The Freedom of the Christian Man." And then I would believe again that the virtues of simple faith would always triumph over intolerance. Whenever I had enough money saved, I would go to Germany, to Eisenach, to the room in the Wartburg where Luther worked. "A mighty fortress is our God." But last year when I was there I saw the Nazis. I saw old friends of mine, living in terror—some of them because they have Jewish blood—some just because they retain a sense of common decency. Even ministers of the gospel—afraid that if they preached the true devotion to God's word they would go into concentration camps. I saw men marching—marching—marching.

(MIRANDA *rises and begins to dust again.*)

Day and night, singing "Today we own Germany—tomorrow the whole world." They didn't know where they were marching to. They didn't care. They had been drilled and lectured down to the ·level where marching itself was enough. I was with one of my friends, an old musician like me, and we were looking from the windows of his house. Across the street a truckload of young Nazis had pulled up and they were wrecking the home of a Jewish dentist. They wanted to take the gold he used to put in people's teeth. They were doing it systematically, as the Germans do everything. And my friend whispered to me—for he did not dare raise his voice, even in his own home—he said, "They say they are doing this to fight Bolshevism. It is a lie! For they *are* Bolshevism!" And that is the truth. . . . "Today we own Germany, tomorrow the whole world." Including Russia.

MIRANDA (*coming close to him*)

They can't win, Uncle Waldemar.

UNCLE WALDEMAR (*rises and looks out the window*)

Can *we* prevent them from winning? All we can do is defend ourselves to the end. And then they sweep over us to the next goal—and the next——

MIRANDA

You're a good Christian, Uncle Waldemar. You have to believe that they can't win.

UNCLE WALDEMAR (*passionately*)

I can believe in the coming of the anti-Christ. I can believe in the Apocalpyse. "And Satan shall be loosed out of his prison, and shall go out to deceive the nations which are in the four quarters of the earth."

(MIRANDA *dusts the keys of the piano.* ERIK *comes in at the right. He is wearing the uniform of the ski troops.*)

ERIK

Mother—I have to leave in a few minutes— (*He sees her face as she looks at him. There is a long pause.* ERIK *takes off his hat. Finally she crosses to him.*) Mother, I'm going into the north with a detachment of ski troops. I don't know just where we're being sent, but we're to assemble at the station in an hour.

MIRANDA

Is Kaatri going with you?

ERIK

No. She'll be at the station, but she doesn't know yet what they want her to do. I have to fix up my pack right away.

MIRANDA

You'll want some food for the journey. I'll get some for you. . . .

(*He kisses her cheek.*)
Whatever we have in the kitchen——

ERIK

Thank you, Mother. (*He goes out at the right.*)

MIRANDA (*to* UNCLE WALDEMAR)

If I'd only known about this sooner, I'd have gotten some things in. I—I suppose there's some canned stuff. . . . (*She seems helpless, despairing.*)

UNCLE WALDEMAR (*rising*)

I'll help you look, Miranda.
(*As they both go toward the dining room.*)
I'm sure there are plenty of good things we can find for Erik.

KAARLO'S VOICE (*from off, right*)

Miranda!
(MIRANDA *stops short.* UNCLE WALDEMAR *goes on out, into the kitchen.*)

MIRANDA

Kaarlo?

KAARLO (*entering*)

Yes. Miranda—look who has come back to Helsinki! Mr. Corween, you remember him?
(DAVE *comes in and goes to* MIRANDA.)

MIRANDA

Of course.

DAVE

I'm so glad to see you again, Mrs. Valkonen.

KAARLO

I just met him. He arrived only this morning, and he was on his way to see us. (*He goes to her and kisses her.*) It was awful, not being able to telephone?—But you're all right?

MIRANDA

Yes.

KAARLO

And Erik?

MIRANDA

Yes. He's here. He——

KAARLO

But—sit down, Mr. Corween. What will you have to drink?

MIRANDA

Kaarlo——

KAARLO (*to* DAVE)

Excuse me. Yes, my dear——

MIRANDA

Kaarlo! Erik is going into the army. He's upstairs, now, packing his things.

KAARLO

Where is he going?

MIRANDA

I don't know. Into the north somewhere. (MIRANDA *goes to* DAVE.) Do you think there will be much fighting in the north, Mr. Corween?

DAVE

You know more about the situation than I do, Mrs. Valkonen.

MIRANDA

You'll forgive me, Mr. Corween. I have something to do. .

DAVE

Of course.

(MIRANDA *goes out into the kitchen.*)
I think you'd like me to go, Dr. Valkonen.

KAARLO

No, no. Sit down, sit down. Are you going to stay here for a while in Helsinki—or is this another flying visit?

DAVE (*sitting*)

I don't know how long I shall stay. It—it all depends.

KAARLO

You'll be broadcasting from here?

DAVE

Oh, yes, Doctor. The American public likes to be kept in touch with all that's going on.

KAARLO

That's good. We like to keep in touch with them. (*He is making a gallant attempt to sustain polite conversation.*) We heard your broadcasts from Warsaw. They were brilliant.

DAVE

Thank you. I can't say I enjoyed them very much.

KAARLO (*sitting—quietly*)

It was tragic, wasn't it!

DAVE

Yes, it was. Dr. Valkonen, I know that this is no time for me to be bothering you or your wife, but——

KAARLO

You are more than welcome here, my dear friend.

DAVE

I know that, Doctor. But there's something I want to say.

KAARLO

Yes?

DAVE

I saw Jim Walsh at the American Legation.

KAARLO

Yes—yes.

DAVE

He is very fond of you and Mrs. Valkonen.

KAARLO

Thank you.

DAVE

As he should be. He asked me to beg you to leave Finland at once.

(KAARLO *looks at him.*)

He can arrange everything. A ship has been chartered next Tuesday from Goteborg, for New York. It is to take hundreds of American refugees. Mr. Walsh can arrange passage for you and Mrs. Valkonen. He can get you to Sweden by plane. But —he must know about it at once.

Kaarlo

Well, now—that's very kind of Mr. Walsh, especially when he's so busy.

Dave (*earnestly*)

I hope you will do it, Dr. Valkonen.

Kaarlo

You mean—go?

Dave

Yes—and at once.

Kaarlo

I am needed here for the time being. There is a great shortage of doctors. All of the young men in all the hospitals are going to the front, for service with the army medical corps. There will be many more casualties here from air raids.

Dave

It's not my business to say so, Doctor—but that isn't suitable work for a winner of the Nobel prize.

Kaarlo (*with great sadness*)

It is not suitable work for any member of the human race, Mr. Corween. But some one must do it.

DAVE

I realize that you're a patriotic citizen of this country——

KAARLO

I am not a patriotic citizen of this country, Mr. Corween. I hope I am aware of the fact that "patriotism" as now practiced is one of the most virulent manifestations of evil.

DAVE

Yes, Doctor. That's just what I mean. You're a citizen of the world. You're of importance to the whole world, not just to these few gallant men who are going to fight and die for Finland. . . . Oh—I know it's presumptuous of me to be talking to you. But—I beg you, please, for God's sake, while you still have the chance, go to a country where you can carry on your work—your own fight —to bring men to consciousness——

KAARLO

But I shall carry on that work as long as I live, Mr. Corween—wherever I am.

DAVE

As long as you live! I'm sorry if I seem unduly emotional about it, Doctor—but—I have seen too many men of intellectual distinction forced into uniform, forced to pick up guns and shoot because they had discovered that their intelligence was impotent to cope with brutal reality. *You* may be forced into that situation, Dr. Valkonen. You who have devoted yourself to discovering the inward defenses of man. You may find yourself, crouching behind a sand-bag, shooting at an illiterate Russian peasant.

KAARLO

Yes, Mr. Corween. You know whereof you speak. And I should be the last to dispute you. Now—we feel like heroes, strong in the armor of the justice of our own cause. Soon—we may be corpses. It is all very foolish—very temporary. But, you see, I am accustomed to this sort of thing. In my youth, this country was ruled by the Romanovs. I survived that oppression. I am prepared to endure it again. Let the forces of evil engulf us. If the truth is in here, my friend——

(*He taps his heart.* MIRANDA *comes in with* ERIK.)

MIRANDA

Kaarlo, Erik must go now.

DAVE (*he knows he must get out before the possibly painful farewells are said*)

I'm afraid I must go now. (*To* ERIK.) How do you do? I—I have to get back to the hotel, to stand by for orders from New York. I'll be at the Kamp, Mrs. Valkonen, and I hope I'll see you soon again. Good-bye, Doctor. Good-bye, Mrs. Valkonen.

ERIK

Good-bye.

MIRANDA

You must come to see us often.

DAVE

Thank you, I shall. Good-bye. Good luck.

(DAVE *goes out. There is a moment of tense silence. No one knows quite what to say.*)

KAARLO (*to* ERIK)

You're leaving now?

ERIK

Yes, Father. We're to be at the station at five o'clock. I—I'd better go at once. I don't want to be late. (*To* MIRANDA.) Where's Uncle Waldemar?

MIRANDA

He's bringing the food for you from the kitchen. You'll be able to say good-bye to him on the way out.

KAARLO

I take it you know what you're doing—what chances you have of accomplishing anything.

ERIK

Yes, Father. I think I know about that.

KAARLO

Very well, then. There's nothing I can say to you but good-bye.

ERIK (*to* KAARLO)

Father, before I go, I want you to know that I'm sorry for you. I think I understand what this is for you. It's worse for you than it is for any of us. But—if it's any consolation to you—I hope you'll remember—you have a son who at least obeys the Fourth Commandment. I honor my father and my mother.

(*The emotion of this is a bit too much for* ERIK. *He hides his face in his hands.* KAARLO *leans over and kisses him tenderly.*)

KAARLO

Go on, go on, Erik.
(ERIK *turns from him toward* MIRANDA.)

MIRANDA

I'll go to the door with you, darling.
(*They go out.* KAARLO *is alone. He goes to a chair at the extreme left, sits down, looks out the window, lost, helpless.* MIRANDA *returns and sits on the couch at the right.*)

KAARLO (*almost angrily*)

I suppose you want to weep now? Then you'd better go to our room and get it over with.

MIRANDA

What good will it do to weep? I've never in my life understood what it is to enjoy the luxury of a good cry. (*She rises suddenly.*) I'm going to the kitchen.

KAARLO

What for?

MIRANDA

I don't know. I have to start trying to learn how to cook.

(*She goes out.* KAARLO *looks after her miserably. After a moment,* UNCLE WALDEMAR *comes in.*)

UNCLE WALDEMAR

Kaarlo. . . . Kaarlo——

KAARLO

Yes.

UNCLE WALDEMAR

Dr. Ziemssen is here.

KAARLO

Dr. Ziemssen?

UNCLE WALDEMAR

He has come to say good-bye. He is going back to Germany.

KAARLO

Oh. . . . Very well, I'll see him.

UNCLE WALDEMAR (*going off at the right*)

Come in, Dr. Ziemssen.

(DR. ZIEMSSEN *comes in. He is wearing his overcoat, carrying his hat and walking stick.* UNCLE WALDEMAR *closes the door behind him.*)

KAARLO

I'm delighted you came in. Let me take your coat.

ZIEMSSEN

Thank you, no, Herr Doktor. I can stay but a short time.

KAARLO

Please sit down.

ZIEMSSEN

I know this is not an opportune moment. I saw Erik go. I saluted him—a splendid young soldier. You have good cause to be proud.

KAARLO (*as they sit on the sofa*)

Thank you, Dr. Ziemssen. I'm sorry to hear you're going. I've greatly enjoyed our discussions at the Institute. But—I can well understand that this is not the place for you under the circumstances.

ZIEMSSEN (*seriously*)

It is not the place for you, either, Dr. Valkonen. I advise you also to go.

KAARLO

Go?

ZIEMSSEN

Leave Finland. Leave Europe at once!

KAARLO

Why is everybody ordering me out of my home? Mr. Corween was here also telling me I must leave.

ZIEMSSEN

Mr. Corween is a remarkably well-informed man. He is aware of the inevitable outcome of this war, as you yourself must be, Herr Doktor. Oh—I have all admiration for the little Finnish army. But two hundred thousand against ten million——

KAARLO

Yes, we will be conquered, as we have been conquered before. And then we will be ruled from Moscow—as we were formerly ruled from Petersburg. But as I was just saying to Mr. Corween, I shall continue with my experiments.

ZIEMSSEN

Dr. Valkonen—I must warn you—you are making a serious mistake!

KAARLO

Mistake?

ZIEMSSEN

You are judging this situation in terms of the past.

KAARLO

One can only judge by one's own experience.

ZIEMSSEN

Precisely. Your own experience is misleading.

KAARLO

In what way, Dr. Ziemssen?

ZIEMSSEN

That is just what I wish to tell you. You think our enemies are these—these Communists who now invade your country?

KAARLO

Yes. That is what I think.

ZIEMSSEN

The Russians think so, too, but they are wrong. *We* are your enemies, Herr Doktor. This Finnish incident is one little item in our vast scheme. We make good use of our esteemed allies of the Soviet Union. All the little communist cells, in labor movements, youth movements, in all nations—they are now working for *us*, although they may not know it. Communism is a good laxative to loosen the constricted bowels of democracy. When it has served that purpose, it will disappear down the sewer with the excrement that must be purged.

KAARLO

It seems to me, Dr. Ziemssen, you are talking with extremely undiplomatic frankness.

ZIEMSSEN

I know I can do so to you, Herr Doktor. You are a scientist. You are accustomed to face facts —even those facts which to the ordinary, dull mind are too terrible to contemplate.

KAARLO

What is it you are threatening, Doctor? What is going to happen to Finland?

ZIEMSSEN

You do not know the whole story of what happened to Poland!

(KAARLO *looks at him, rises, and walks away.*) You will hear the Pope in Rome weeping publicly

and proclaiming that the Polish nation will rise
again. I assure you it will not rise again, because,
as a nation, it is dead. The same is true of every
nation that we conquer; we shall see to it that none
of them will ever rise again. Today, the remnants
of the Polish people are scattered all the way from
the Rhine to the Pacific coast of Siberia. This is a
process of annihilation. It is a studied technique,
and it was not invented in Moscow. You will find
the blueprints of it, not in *Das Kapital*, but in
Mein Kampf. It is all there for you to read. It
involves, first, liquidation of all leaders of thought
—political, religious, economic, intellectual.

(KAARLO *sits down. He seems to slump.*)

Among the masses—the difficult ones are killed—
the weaklings are allowed to die of starvation—the
strong ones are enslaved.

KAARLO

You are an anthropologist—a man of learning,
Dr. Ziemssen. Do you approve of this technique?

ZIEMSSEN

Naturally, I regret the necessity for it. But I
admit the necessity. And so must you, Dr. Valkonen. Remember that every great state of the
past in its stages of construction has required
slavery. Today, the greatest world state is in
process of formation. There is a great need for
slave labor. And—these Finns and Scandinavians
would be useful. They are strong; they have
great capacity for endurance. Is that brutal—

ruthless? Yes. But I am now talking to a scientist, not a snivelling sentimentalist. Vivisection has been called brutal, ruthless—but it is necessary for the survival of man. So it is necessary that inferior races be considered merely as animals. . . . Do you believe me, Herr Doktor?

KAARLO

I believe you. Although—still talking as one scientist to another—I cannot help wondering just how you establish proof that these other races are inferior, especially when you know it is a lie.

ZIEMSSEN

Of course it is a lie, biologically. But we can prove it by the very simple expedient of asserting our own superiority—just as the Romans did before they decayed—and the Anglo-Saxons, before *they* decayed. View this objectively, Herr Doktor, and then you will be able to proceed with your experiments. You have made important progress in an important field—conditioning men to their environment. That can be of extraordinary value to us in the future. You can help to postpone, perhaps indefinitely, the time when *we* will be conquered by decay. But, first—you must accept the theory of the new world state, for that *is* the environment of the future. If you refuse to accept, and stay here and attempt to resist destiny, you will die.

KAARLO

Where can one go to escape this world state?

ZIEMSSEN (*smiles*)

An intelligent question, Herr Doktor. I assure
you that the United States is secure for the present. It may continue so for a long time, if the
Americans refrain from interfering with us in
Mexico and South America and Canada. And I
believe they will refrain. They are now showing far
greater intelligence in that respect than ever before. They are learning to mind their own shrink-
ing business.

KAARLO

I appreciate your motives in warning me, Dr.
Ziemssen. And I understand that all you have told
me is confidential.

ZIEMSSEN (*laughing*)

You *are* an innocent, my friend! Nothing that
I have said is confidential. You may repeat it all.
And you will not be believed. There is the proof
of our superiority—that our objectives are so vast
that our pigmy-minded enemies simply have not
the capacity to believe them. They are eager to
accept the big lies we give them, because they cannot comprehend the big truth. (*Rises.*) And the
big truth is this: For the first time since the whole
surface of the earth became known, one dynamic
race is on the march to occupy that surface and
rule it! When you have absorbed that huge conception, you will find that your own theories can
be adjusted to it. And now I must go. (*He extends his hand to* KAARLO.) But I advise you to

make haste, Herr Doktor. Finland's only lines of communication are through Sweden and Norway. We have many means of cutting those lines. Good-bye, Herr Doktor. I said good-bye. I hope we part friends. (*He goes to the door.*)

(KAARLO *nods as he shakes hands with* DR. ZIEMSSEN.)
My compliments to Frau Valkonen. Good-bye. (*He goes.*)

UNCLE WALDEMAR'S VOICE (*heard offstage*)
Good-bye, Dr. Ziemssen.

ZIEMSSEN'S VOICE
Good-bye, Herr Sederstrum. I have so enjoyed your music.
(KAARLO *crosses and stands behind the sofa.* UNCLE WALDEMAR *enters, switches on lights, goes immediately to the windows and starts closing the black curtains.* KAARLO *looks toward the kitchen.*)

KAARLO
Uncle Waldemar—Uncle Waldemar——

UNCLE WALDEMAR
Yes. . . . What is it? (*Having fixed the windows,* UNCLE WALDEMAR *turns to* KAARLO.)

KAARLO
Get your hat and coat on.

UNCLE WALDEMAR
What for?

KAARLO

I want you to go to the American Legation and
see Mr. Walsh. Tell him that Mrs. Valkonen will
leave on that ship Mr. Corween told me about. I
believe it sails from Goteborg on Tuesday. He
must make all the necessary arrangements at once.
Find out what is the earliest possible moment she
can leave for Sweden. Ask him if it is safe by
aeroplane.

UNCLE WALDEMAR

You're sending Miranda away—alone?

KAARLO

Yes. Be quiet. She's right there in the kitchen.

UNCLE WALDEMAR

You think you can persuade her to do this?

KAARLO

I have to persuade her, and if necessary, you
will help me. You know what has happened to
Poland.

UNCLE WALDEMAR

Yes, I know. But—Miranda doesn't care about
those things. She doesn't believe them.

KAARLO

I didn't believe them either. . . . But—I'll find
another way of persuading her. If ruthlessness is
the order of this day, then I shall be ruthless, too.
I will tell her I don't want her here. She is of no
use in a time like this.

UNCLE WALDEMAR

That will hurt her more deeply than the Russians ever could.

KAARLO

She will recover from that hurt. Go ahead!

UNCLE WALDEMAR

Very well.

(*He starts to go, but* MIRANDA *enters. She is carrying a tray on which are a coffee pot and cups.*)

MIRANDA

Uncle Waldemar—I made some coffee. Would you like some?

UNCLE WALDEMAR

No, thank you.

MIRANDA

I tasted it. It's quite good.

UNCLE WALDEMAR

Thank you—but I have to go.

MIRANDA

Where?

UNCLE WALDEMAR

I want to have some exercise and fresh air.

MIRANDA

But you've been out all day.

UNCLE WALDEMAR

Even so—I'm going out again.

(*He goes out.* MIRANDA *takes the tray over to the piano and puts it down.*)

MIRANDA

Poor Uncle Waldemar—all this has upset him terribly. . . . Will you have some coffee, Kaarlo?

KAARLO

No, thank you.

MIRANDA

I wish you'd try it.

KAARLO

Later, perhaps. . . . Please sit down.

MIRANDA

What is it, Kaarlo? Do you want to talk about Erik? (*She starts to go out.*)

KAARLO

No—I do not want to talk about Erik. Please sit down.
(*She sits down and looks at him, curiously.*)
I wish to tell you, my dear, that the time has come for you to go home.

MIRANDA

Home? This is my home.

KAARLO

I mean—to your own country. To America.

MIRANDA (*amazed*)

Why?

KAARLO

Because I do not wish you to stay here. Mr. Walsh at the American Legation can make all the necessary arrangements. You will probably leave for Sweden tomorrow—perhaps even tonight. We will hear soon about that. You can then go to Boston and stay with your aunt.

MIRANDA

Will you go with me?

KAARLO

Naturally not. I am needed here. You will stay in America until this business is over.

MIRANDA

And when it *is* over? What then?

KAARLO

Why—you'll come back here, and we'll go right on living as we've always done. I might come to America and fetch you.

MIRANDA

Supposing you were killed?

KAARLO

I—killed? I'm a doctor.

MIRANDA

And do you suppose a Russian in a bombing plane ten thousand feet up can tell the difference

between an ordinary person and a winner of the
Nobel prize?

KAARLO

It is out of the question that I should go. Freud
left Vienna after the Nazi occupation. He went
to London, and he was welcomed there, he was
honored. But—he couldn't speak. He knew that if
he told the truth, it would be printed, and his own
people, still in Austria, would be made to suffer for
it, horribly. . . . So Freud was technically free—
but he was silenced. What did he then have to live
for? Nothing. . . . So he died. . . . No—I will
not leave. You must go alone.

MIRANDA

And if I left here—what would *I* have to live for?

KAARLO

Oh, you'll manage very well in your own great,
secure, distant country.

(*He has been moving about the room. Her eyes
have been following him, questioning him, seeking
him out, with every word, every move.*)

MIRANDA

Kaarlo! Tell me the truth. Why do you want
me to go?

KAARLO

What can you do here? This is a war for the
defense of Finland. It must be fought by the Finnish people.

(*She is staring at him. He is avoiding her gaze.*)

This country becomes an armed camp. Every one
of us knows what he must do, or she must do, and
is trained to do it. Are you trained for anything,
but wearing lovely clothes, being a charming
hostess?

(*She looks at him, helplessly.*)

You are an intelligent woman, Miranda. Reason
this out for yourself. You will see that this is a
time when every one who eats bread must have
worked to earn it. And, God help us, there is only
one form of work that matters now—resistance—
blind, dogged, desperate resistance.

MIRANDA (*rising, and following him*)

You've said yourself—that kind of resistance is
useless.

(*She is trying desperately to score a point. He
is trying desperately to avoid being scored on,
though ever conscious of his vulnerability.*)

KAARLO (*angrily*)

You don't know what I've said. Or—if you know
the words, you have less idea of their meaning than
the youngest of the students who hear my lectures
at the Institute. I'm not insulting your courage,
Miranda. Nor your good will. I'm sure you would
like to be useful. But you can't. You know you
can't.

MIRANDA

You think it would be impossible for me to con-
tribute anything—to help in any way?

KAARLO

Why do I have to tell you what you must know yourself?

(MIRANDA *looks at him with a look almost of bitter hostility. She turns and walks away. Unutterably miserable, he looks after her. The artifice of his frigid superiority is beginning to crumple.*) There is no reason for you to be ashamed of this. This is not your country. It is not your war.

MIRANDA

This is the country of my husband and my son.

KAARLO

And do you think Erik and I want you to be caught in these ruins?

MIRANDA

You have no right to speak of Erik! I don't think he would be particularly happy or proud to hear that his mother has scurried to safety at the first sound of a shot fired.

KAARLO

Erik has American blood in his veins. He will understand.

MIRANDA (*flaming*)

Oh! So that's it! His American blood will tell him that it's perfectly reasonable for me to run away. You evidently share Kaatri's opinion of me.

KAARLO (*desperately*)

Don't put words into my mouth that I have not uttered——

MIRANDA (*turning on him, suddenly coming to him*)

Then don't be afraid to come out and say what you mean. It's obvious that you don't want me here, because I'm incompetent—I'm a parasite—I'm a non-essential. In all these years that we've been together nothing has happened to disturb the lovely serenity of our home. And now comes this great calamity. And immediately you decide that you don't want me—you don't need me.

KAARLO

I didn't say that!

MIRANDA

Then what did you say?

(KAARLO *is obviously making a last effort to control himself.*)

KAARLO

Miranda! You don't understand why I want you to go!

MIRANDA

It makes no difference to me whether I understand it or not. There's one thing I do know, and you'd better know it, too: I am not going. Probably, you *don't* need me. You have important work to do—and I'm sure that's enough, for you. But

the time may come when Erik might need me, and
when that time comes, I intend to be here——

KAARLO

No, please—for God's sake—don't keep on bringing Erik into it! Wasn't it bad enough to see him
going away like that, in his uniform? That poor,
hopeful, defenseless child! (*He sees that he has
hurt her, terribly, with that.*) Oh—I'm sorry, darling. You must see that I've been making a desperate attempt to drive you to safety with lies.
It's no use. You always can make me tell the truth.
The real trouble is—you've had too much confidence in me. How could you know that I was living
in a dream—a beautiful, wishful dream in which
you played your own unsubstantial but exciting
part? And now—there is war—and our own son
goes to fight—and I wake up to discover that
reality itself is a hideous nightmare. . . . I
shouldn't be talking to you like this, Miranda. I'm
frightened.

MIRANDA

You can never be afraid to say anything to me,
darling.

KAARLO

I have suddenly realized what and where I am.
I am a man working in the apparent security of a
laboratory. I am working on a theory so tentative
that it may take hundreds of years of research,
and generations of workers, to prove it. I am trying to defeat insanity—degeneration of the human

race. . . . And then—a band of pyromaniacs enters the building in which I work. And that building is the world—the whole planet—not just Finland. They set fire to it. What can I do? Until that fire is put out, there can be no peace—no freedom from fear—no hope of progress for mankind. . . . Every day that we hold them off—will only serve to increase the terror of the vengeance which must surely descend upon us. All the pathetic survivors of this war will have to pay in torture for the heroism of the dead. And it isn't just us—not just this one little breed that wants to be free. This is a war for everybody—yes—even for the scientists who thought themselves immune behind their test tubes. (*He looks into her eyes again.*) Darling! I can stand this ordeal if I know it is only for myself. I can stand it if I know you are safe—that you are beyond their reach. . . . I love you. That is the only reality left to me. I love you.

(*They are in each other's arms. For a moment, they are silent.*)

MIRANDA

Then I can stand it, too, darling, whatever it is. I can stand it as long as I know that you love me —that you do need me—that I am essential, after all. Even if I am a woman who is nothing but a woman. Even at a time when the whole life of the world is marching with men. . . .

(*They hold each other, closely. After a moment, she rises.*)
Now come and have some coffee.

(*They cross to the piano. She feels the coffee pot.*)

It's not very warm.

KAARLO

It's no matter, darling. I'm sure it's good.

(*She is pouring the coffee.*)

CURTAIN

SCENE IV

The same. New Year's Day, 1940. Noon. There is a Christmas tree. There are many decorations on the tree, including a wide, white ribbon on which is an inscription in Finnish. At the top of the tree is a star.

UNCLE WALDEMAR *is at the piano playing something surprisingly spirited and gay.* KAARLO *comes in. He wears the uniform coat of a Colonel in the Medical Corps, but otherwise he is in civilian clothes. He is buttoning up the coat. As he glances back into the mirror, he looks rather sheepish and self-conscious.* UNCLE WALDEMAR *looks at him.*

KAARLO

Well—Uncle Waldemar—haven't you anything to say about my new uniform?

UNCLE WALDEMAR

What should I say? I've seen thousands of uniforms lately. They all look the same.

KAARLO (*laughs*)

I know. But—for some reason—when you see one on yourself, it seems to look better.

UNCLE WALDEMAR (*stops playing, rises*)

Are you trying to fool me, Kaarlo?

KAARLO

Fool you? Why should I——?

UNCLE WALDEMAR

You want me to think you are proud to be going?

KAARLO (*gravely*)

No, Uncle Waldemar. (*He looks off to the kitchen, and then speaks confidentially.*) When Erik went—I—I thought our world had come to an end. Since then—I have been struggling to adjust myself—to find in all this tragedy some intimation of hope for the future.

UNCLE WALDEMAR (*tenderly*)

I know, Kaarlo.

KAARLO

This (*indicates his uniform coat*) represents the final stage in that attempt at adjustment. It is like the moment when a scientist knows he can no longer experiment with guinea pigs—he must now test his theories on human life itself. It is kill or cure.

UNCLE WALDEMAR

What are those ribbons you are wearing?

KAARLO

The order of St. Ann with Swords—the Cross of St. George's.

UNCLE WALDEMAR

You're going into the Mannerheim Line wearing Russian decorations?

KAARLO

Why not? I won them. Or—at any rate—
they were given to me. You think I should leave
them off?

(MIRANDA *comes in from the kitchen with a
tray on which are a pitcher of eggnog and five
punch glasses. She sees* KAARLO's *coat.*)

MIRANDA

What is that you are wearing?

KAARLO

It is my uniform coat. I was just trying it on.

MIRANDA

What for? What do you want with a uniform?

KAARLO

Of course I should have one. I'm a Colonel in
the Army Medical Corps.

MIRANDA

Now don't tell me you want to look impressive.
Why have you suddenly got a uniform?

KAARLO

Because I have to, Miranda. I'm going to
Viipuri.

MIRANDA (*shocked*)

When are you going?

KAARLO

This afternoon, I believe. What is that on the tray you brought in?

MIRANDA

It's eggnog. I promised Dave Corween I'd make some to celebrate New Year's. Why are they sending you to Viipuri?

KAARLO

Nobody is sending me, Miranda. I'm going because I wish to. More hospital space has to be provided there, and I want to see that the work is done efficiently.

MIRANDA

Why haven't you told me about this before? You knew about it, Uncle Waldemar?

UNCLE WALDEMAR

He told me only today.

KAARLO

Now really, Miranda. This is not to be taken so seriously. I am not going very far away, and I shall probably be back within a fortnight. In fact, Dave Corween is going with me and a Polish officer named Rutkowski. Dave is to broadcast from Viipuri. That proves there's no danger. (*He starts to go out at the right.*)

MIRANDA

How do you get to Viipuri?

KAARLO

I go in style . . . in that new American ambulance that just arrived from France. (*He goes out taking off his coat.*)

MIRANDA (*looking after* KAARLO)

He was afraid to tell me—wasn't he, Uncle Waldemar?

UNCLE WALDEMAR

Kaarlo always likes to avoid unpleasant subjects . . . outside his laboratory.

MIRANDA

Is there something serious happening?

UNCLE WALDEMAR

Well—you know, Miranda—there is still war. They still attack.

MIRANDA

But everything's going well for us, isn't it?

UNCLE WALDEMAR

We're alive. That's more than any one expected.

MIRANDA

Why do they want more hospitals at Viipuri? I thought there weren't many wounded.

UNCLE WALDEMAR

That is because now most of the wounded are frozen to death before they can be brought in. When warmer weather comes—the fighting will be different. They will need hospitals—especially on the isthmus.

(*She considers this dreadful thought for a moment.*)

MIRANDA (*desperately*)

Oh, God—Uncle Waldemar. Why don't we hear from Erik? He has been gone a whole month—*why* don't we hear?

(UNCLE WALDEMAR *comes to her.*)

UNCLE WALDEMAR

We know Erik is well. Kaarlo sees every casualty list—including even those who are sick. It's just that up there in the Arctic there is not much chance of sending letters.

(*The doorbell is heard.*)

MIRANDA

There's the doorbell.

UNCLE WALDEMAR

I'll go, Miranda. (UNCLE WALDEMAR *goes out.*)

(VOICES *can be heard off at the right*)
How do you do, Mr. Corween?

DAVE (*off*)

How do you do, sir?

UNCLE WALDEMAR (*off*)

Happy New Year!

DAVE (*off*)

Happy New Year to you, sir!

UNCLE WALDEMAR (*off*)

Go right in.

DAVE (*off*)

Thank you. (DAVE *comes in. He is dressed for a cold journey.*)

MIRANDA

Dave! Happy New Year!

DAVE

Happy New Year, Mrs. Valkonen.

MIRANDA (*pointing to the tray*)

I've kept my promise about the eggnog.

DAVE

I'm afraid I'm going to overtax your hospitality. There are four other boys here, all going up with the ambulance.

MIRANDA

Oh! Bring them all in.

DAVE

Thank you. (*He calls off.*) Come in, boys. Come in, Major.

(MAJOR RUTKOWSKI *comes in. He is a tired, tragic young Polish officer. He is followed almost at once by* JOE BURNETT, BEN GICHNER *and* FRANK OLMSTEAD. JOE *is tall, lean, wearing a smart, new aviator's uniform;* BEN *is stout and cheerful;* FRANK, *young, sensitive and serious-minded. Both* BEN *and* FRANK *wear uniforms of the American Ambulance Corps, with Red Cross insignia on the sleeves.)*

DAVE

Mrs. Valkonen—this is Major Rutkowski.

RUTKOWSKI (*bows*)

Madame.

MIRANDA

How do you do?

DAVE

And this is the American Expeditionary Force in Finland. Joe Burnett of Haverford, Pa.——

MIRANDA (*shaking hands with each in turn*)

How do you do?

DAVE

Ben Gichner of Cincinnati.

MIRANDA

I'm very glad to see you.

DAVE

And Frank Olmstead of San Francisco. Mrs. Valkonen of New Bedford.

MIRANDA

Happy New Year!

JOE

Thank you, Mrs. Valkonen.

FRANK

Thank you.

BEN

And a very happy New Year to you, Madame.

MIRANDA

I have some eggnog, gentlemen——

(*Their faces light up.*)

In the midst of war we still have some milk and eggs and rye whiskey and even a little cream. You start serving it, Dave—while I get some more glasses. Sit down, everybody. (*She goes out through the dining room.*)

DAVE (*crossing*)

Come on, Joe.

(JOE *and* FRANK *follow* DAVE *across.* BEN *and* RUTKOWSKI *are looking about the room.*)

Now, boys, remember. No remarks about the horrors of war. I'm afraid Mrs. Valkonen feels pretty badly about her husband going.

JOE

We'll be tactful, Dave.

RUTKOWSKI (*quietly*)

A lovely house. This would be the house of good people in any country.

BEN

It's got a sort of nice, Victorian quality. I thought everything in Finland was moderne.

FRANK (*who is looking at the photographs on the piano*)

Look, Joe. . . . Doctor Jung, Alexis Carrel, President Masaryk——

DAVE (*bringing drinks across to* RUTKOWSKI *and* BEN)

Here you are, Major Rutkowski. Nourishing and stimulating—but apt to be dangerous.

(FRANK *is standing by the piano, playing a few bars of a swing tune.*)

MIRANDA (*offstage*)

Have you tried it yet?

DAVE

We were waiting for you, Mrs. Valkonen.

(MIRANDA *re-enters with a tray holding more glasses.* BEN *and* RUTKOWSKI *rise.* DAVE *takes the tray from her, goes to the serving table and pours drinks for* MIRANDA *and himself.*)

MIRANDA

Here you are—here are the glasses. (*To* FRANK.) Was that you playing?

FRANK (*diffidently*)

I wouldn't call it playing.

MIRANDA

It is wonderful.

BEN

Come on, Dave. I think you ought to make a little speech in behalf of all of us.

DAVE

I'm not at my best without a mike and a coast-to-coast hook-up. (*He raises his glass and addresses* MIRANDA.) However, we want to tell you we're glad to be here, enjoying your gracious hospitality, and we hope that this New Year will bring you and yours health and happiness.

MIRANDA (*as the circle of men gathers about her*)

Why, that was a charming speech, Dave. I wish the same to you, all of you, and I welcome you to this house and this country. And I'd like to sing the Polish national anthem and "The Star-Spangled Banner," but I don't know the words of either.

DAVE (*laughs*)

That's all right, Mrs. Valkonen. Neither do we. (*They all drink.*)

JOE

It's magnificent.

DAVE

Mrs. Valkonen, it's better even than the Parker House Punch.

BEN

Frankly, I love it.

FRANK

So do I.

RUTKOWSKI

I've never tasted anything quite like it before—but I'm glad to be introduced.

MIRANDA

Thank you—thank you. (*To* FRANK.) Do go on playing. Help yourselves as long as it lasts. There are American cigarettes.

(MIRANDA *sits on the sofa.* FRANK *goes to the piano and plays.*)

DAVE

Everybody admires your house, Mrs. Valkonen.

BEN

Yes. I was just saying, it has a nice, old-fashioned quality.

RUTKOWSKI

It is so graceful.

MIRANDA

I'm glad you see it with the Christmas tree. That always makes it more cheerful.

FRANK (*stops playing*)

May I ask—what is the inscription on that ribbon?

MIRANDA

It's Finnish for "Glory to God in the highest and, on earth, peace, good will to men." (*A pause.*) We have that on the tree every Christmas. It's a tradition in this country.

KAARLO (*calling from off stage, at the right*)

I'll be with you in a moment, gentlemen. I have to assemble my kit.

MIRANDA (*calling to him*)

Can I help you, Kaarlo?

KAARLO (*off*)

No, thank you, my dear. Is the eggnog good, gentlemen?

DAVE

It's superb!

BEN

We're in no hurry to leave, Doctor. We're having a fine time.

MIRANDA

Have all you gentlemen just arrived in Helsinki?

BEN

We got here yesterday, ma'am. . . . I mean, Frank Olmstead and Joe Burnett and me. We came by ship from Paris to Norway. Major Rutkowski has been here since November.

MIRANDA

Had you been in the war in Poland, Major?

RUTKOWSKI

Yes, Madame, but it lasted only three weeks. I was in the cavalry.

MIRANDA

How did you manage to get here?

RUTKOWSKI

From Riga, Madame. The survivors of my regiment were driven over the Lithuanian border. I worked my way to Helsinki intending to go on through Sweden to France to join the Polish Legion there. But——

MIRANDA

But—there was a war here, so you didn't have to look any further.

RUTKOWSKI

Yes, Madame.

MIRANDA

We used to listen to Dave when he was broadcasting from Warsaw, describing the incredible heroism during the siege. Day after day we'd hear the German official radio announcing that Warsaw had fallen and then, late at night, we'd hear the government's station, playing Chopin's "Polonaise," to let us know they were still there.

BEN

We heard it, too, in Paris. It was thrilling.

DAVE

What were you doing in Paris, Ben—if it isn't too personal a question?

BEN

I was employed there! I worked for the American Express Company. I was a travel salesman. (*He turns to* MIRANDA.) I've sold many tours to picturesque Scandinavia and the Baltic, but this is my first visit to these parts.

MIRANDA

We're very glad that you're here.

BEN

Thank you.

MIRANDA

And what were you doing, Mr. Burnett?

JOE

For the last two years I've been in jail—in one of General Franco's mediæval dungeons.

MIRANDA

You fought in Spain?

JOE

Yes, Mrs. Valkonen.

MIRANDA

Why, you're a hero, Mr. Burnett.

JOE

No, Mrs. Valkonen. No hero. Just a bum. I went to Spain only because I was kicked out of Princeton.

DAVE

What for?

JOE

For throwing forward passes in chapel.

BEN

All fliers are a little crazy. Now, you take Frank and me—we're sane. We're ambulance drivers.

We're non-combatants, we hope. We'll have a good safe view of this country. And what I want to see most is some of those ski troops.

(DAVE *looks at him, sharply.*)

Will there be any of them around Viipuri?

JOE

They're all up in the north, aren't they?

MIRANDA

Yes. They're in the north. (*Noticing* JOE's *empty glass.*) Let me get you some more. (*She takes* JOE's *glass, rises and crosses to the serving table.*)

DAVE (*rising*)

You won't see much action around Viipuri. The Mannerheim Line is just about as quiet as the Western Front.

MIRANDA

Dave is always reassuring—at least when he's talking to me. But I think he's less optimistic when he's broadcasting the news.

DAVE

That's only because I have to dramatize things for the radio audience. They like to be scared. In fact, every night, when I'm on the air, I have to remember that I'm in competition with a thriller program called "Renfrew of the Mounted."

FRANK

I used to listen to that program. Renfrew always gets his man.

(MIRANDA *looks at* FRANK, *surprised at his first contribution to the conversation.*)

MIRANDA

Did Dave say you lived in San Francisco?

FRANK

Yes, Mrs. Valkonen.

MIRANDA

And how long have you been away from home?

FRANK

I came abroad just last summer. I was going to the Sorbonne in Paris.

MIRANDA

Oh! You're a student.

FRANK

Yes, I am. I had an exchange scholarship from my own school, Leland Stanford.

MIRANDA

You must be brilliant! What sort of things were you studying?

FRANK

Well—I particularly wanted to study French verse forms. I realize it sounds pretty ridiculous——

BEN

The terrible truth is that Frank wants to be a poet. (BEN *has to laugh at that.*)

MIRANDA

Now, really—I don't see anything to laugh at.

FRANK

Perhaps you would if you could read any of my attempts.

MIRANDA

I'd love to read some of your poetry. When I was a young girl, my greatest hero was Rupert Brooke. Maybe now that you're here—and have all this experience—maybe you'll write as he did. "Honour has come back, as a king to earth, And paid his subjects with a royal wage; and Nobleness walks in our ways again; and we have come into our heritage."

FRANK

I'm afraid I could never write like Rupert Brooke, even if I were that good. He was always singing of the heroism of war.

MIRANDA

Oh! And you see it as unheroic?

FRANK

Yes, Mrs. Valkonen. I do.

BEN

In addition to being a poet—Frank is also a rabid pacifist.

MIRANDA

I'm glad to hear it. My husband is a pacifist,

too. You must have a talk with him while you're driving to Viipuri.

FRANK

I hope I have that privilege.

BEN

I've been a pacifist myself, in my time. I used to think, I'll never let my children grow up to get into this mass murder. But now I've got to the stage of figuring I ought to help put the murderers out of business *before* my children grow up and have to fight 'em themselves.

DAVE

Have you got any children, Ben?

BEN

No. It was all hypothetical.

MIRANDA

But you came here, to Finland. You came through mine fields and submarines, didn't you?

FRANK

Yes, we did.

MIRANDA

What made you come through all that into this little war?

FRANK

Because I'm a crazy fool, that's why.

MIRANDA

That's interesting. How many crazy fools do you suppose there are in America?

DAVE

I can name four hundred and seventy-three of my own acquaintance.

BEN

The pioneers were fools. And as for that goof Columbus—why didn't *he* stay home and mind his own business? (*He is crossing to help himself to another glass of eggnog.*)

DAVE

Go easy on that punch, Ben. You've got to drive the ambulance.

BEN

You can count on me, Dave.

MIRANDA (*to* RUTKOWSKI)

Have you ever met any Americans before, Major?

RUTKOWSKI

No, I'm sorry, I have not.

MIRANDA

Then this will give you a faint idea.

RUTKOWSKI

I am glad of the opportunity. I have often won-

dered what it could be like to be an American—
to believe, even for a moment, that such things as
peace and security are possible. You see, we have
never been permitted such belief. For us, the sun
rose each morning among our enemies—and it set
among our enemies. And now, it is high noon,
and our enemies have joined together over our
country—and we are gone.

DAVE

It isn't always so completely delightful to be an
American, Major. Sometimes even we have an
uncomfortable feeling of insecurity. I imagine
that Pontius Pilate didn't feel entirely at peace
with himself. He knew that this was a good, just
man, who didn't deserve death. He was against a
crown of thorns on principle. But when they
cried, "Crucify Him!" all Pilate could say was,
"Bring me a basin of water, so that I can wash
my hands of the whole matter."

(KAARLO *comes in, dressed in his uniform.*
UNCLE WALDEMAR *comes after him. All the guests
rise.*)

KAARLO

No—please—don't get up. Gentlemen—this is
my Uncle, Mr. Sederstrum.

UNCLE WALDEMAR

How do you do?

(*All greet him.* MIRANDA *is staring at* KAARLO
in his uniform. He looks at her, smiles lamely.)

KAARLO

Now I'll have a glass of that eggnog. Then I suppose we should go?

RUTKOWSKI (*looking at his watch*)

I'm afraid so.

MIRANDA

Bring a glass for Uncle Waldemar too, Dave.

BEN

To think that I should be going to Viipuri in company with a winner of the Nobel Prize.

KAARLO

I hope we don't get lost on the way. I have no sense of direction whatever. We'll rely on Major Rutkowski to guide us. The Major has been in the Mannerheim Line. Did he tell you about it?

(*This to* MIRANDA, *as she pours his eggnog.*)

MIRANDA

No. He didn't.

KAARLO

Oh—he says it's very dull there. (*He lifts his glass.*) Well, gentlemen, I beg leave to drink to you, our friends from the United States and from Poland.

(*They all move into a circle at the left.*)

DAVE

Thank you, Doctor.

RUTKOWSKI

And long life to the Republic of Finland!

ALL

Hear, hear!

BEN

And to you, Doctor.
(*They drink.*)

KAARLO

Why, Miranda, it's good! Why don't we have
this every day?

(FRANK *goes to the piano and starts playing
"Auld Lang Syne." All sing. . . .* KAATRI *comes
in at the right. She wears the Lotta uniform. She
is very pale.*)

MIRANDA

Kaatri! (*She goes quickly to* KAATRI, *who is
looking wildly around the room at all the stran-
gers.*)

KAATRI

Mrs. Valkonen—I had to see you——

MIRANDA

Have you heard from Erik?

KAATRI

No. But I must talk to you——

DAVE

Come on, boys. Get your coats and hats on.
We'll wait outside, Mrs. Valkonen.

JOE

Certainly.
(*They start to go out.*)

MIRANDA

You'll forgive me, Major Rutkowski. We'll be out in just a moment.

RUTKOWSKI

Of course.
(RUTKOWSKI *goes out at the right after* DAVE, JOE, BEN *and* FRANK.)

MIRANDA

Now, Kaatri dear—what is it?

KAATRI

I've written every day to Erik. I haven't heard from him since that first letter two weeks ago. I've got to see him, Mrs. Valkonen. Don't you think they could give him a little leave?

MIRANDA

He'll surely have leave soon, dear. The Russians have to stop attacking some time. Isn't that so, Kaarlo?

KAARLO

Of course it is. Erik's all right. In fact, he's probably enjoying himself. He likes that energetic life. Now—really—I must go. . . . (*He starts to say good-bye to* UNCLE WALDEMAR.)

KAATRI

No—please, Dr. Valkonen. There's something I have to ask you. I'm going to have a baby.

MIRANDA (*rising*)

Darling. (*She takes her in her arms.*)

KAARLO

Well! I'm very happy to hear it.

KAATRI

I'm not happy. I don't want it! Dr. Valkonen! What can I do to stop it? Please tell me what I can do.

MIRANDA

You're not ashamed, Kaatri? There's nothing for you to be ashamed of.

KAATRI

No—I'm not! But I don't want it. You've got to help me, Dr. Valkonen.

KAARLO

Have you told your family of this?

KAATRI

No. It wouldn't be easy for them to understand, as you do, about Erik and me.

MIRANDA

Why don't you want to have a baby, Kaatri?

KAATRI

I'm working. It would make me useless—just another person to be cared for——

MIRANDA

That's not being useless.

KAATRI

It is now! What good would it be to bring a child into a world like this? He would have no country—no hope. *Please*, Dr. Valkonen. I'm sorry to be troubling you. But—just tell me some doctor that I can see.

KAARLO

You will see Dr. Palm. Miranda—you know him.

MIRANDA

Yes, Kaarlo.

KAARLO

You take Kaatri to see him. Tell him that this is our daughter-in-law, and her baby will be our grandchild.

(KAATRI *looks at him, with terror.*)

Yes, my dear, you are going to have that child.

KAATRI (*hysterical*)

No—no! I won't have it! (*She tries desperately to break away from them.*) I won't have a child born under a curse!

MIRANDA

Quiet, dear. Please. (*She seats* KAATRI *beside her.*)

KAATRI (*making another frantic attempt to get away*)

No! You won't help me. I'll find a doctor——

KAARLO

Do as my wife.tells you, Kaatri! You love Erik, and he loves you. You were willing to be married to him. You have taken responsibility. The highest responsibility! You are not going to evade it.

MIRANDA

Kaatri—Kaatri!
(KAATRI *submits.* KAARLO *leans over her.*)

KAARLO

Whatever happens to our country, your child will not be born under a curse. It will be born to the greatest opportunity that any child has ever known, since the beginning of time. Remember that, and be brave. . . . Now—I can't keep them waiting. Good-bye, Uncle Waldemar. I'll be back soon.

UNCLE WALDEMAR

Yes, Kaarlo. Good-bye.
(*They kiss.* KAARLO *leans over and kisses* KAATRI'S *head. Then he takes* MIRANDA'S *hand. She rises, looks back, motions to* UNCLE WALDE-MAR *to come to* KAATRI.)

KAARLO

Come on, darling.
(*They go out at the right.* KAATRI *is crumpled up on the couch.* UNCLE WALDEMAR *goes over to her, sits down beside her, and takes her in his arms.*)

UNCLE WALDEMAR

Now—don't cry, Kaatri. Pay attention to what Dr. Valkonen told you. *He* knows what he is saying. If he tells you there is good hope, you can believe him.

CURTAIN

SCENE V

Dave Corween's room in the Hotel Kamp in Helsinki.

It is evening.

Upper right is a door leading to the corridor. At the left is a door leading to a bedroom.

The room is in pretty much of a mess. At the right, on a chair, is DAVE's typewriter, with copy paper and carbon strewn about. At the left, is a large table, on which is the same broadcasting apparatus seen in the first scene.

DAVE is at the microphone reading from a typescript before him. GUS is up-stage, left, with his earphones on.

DAVE

In an attempt to surround the main force of the Finnish army on the Karelian Isthmus, the Russians are now making determined attacks across Viipuri Bay. The Mannerheim Line, supposedly impregnable bulwark of Finland's defense, has been shattered. The bombardment of these defenses, and of Viipuri itself, has now reached the terrible total of three hundred thousand shells a day. Looking at the ruination in Viipuri, I could not help thinking of the despairing prophecies made by H. G. Wells in *The Shape of Things to Come*. Here was the awful picture of the collapse

130

of our Western civilization, the beginning of the Age of Frustration. Stores and factories, public libraries, museums, movie theatres—hospitals and schools and homes—all reduced to junk heaps. The Soviet Union is being generous in the expenditure of its ammunition, and extravagantly generous with the life blood of its men. Never again will these workers of the world arise! But in Moscow, the official propaganda bureau broadcasts constantly in Finnish, sending soothing encouragement to this beleaguered little country. Today I heard them say, and I quote, "The Red Army sends greetings to the workers of Finland. The Red Army does not destroy. That is why the workers in every country love the Red Army." And—perhaps, in the end—"love" will conquer all. . . . This is David Corween in Helsinki, returning you now to C. B. S. in New York.

(GUS *switches off the radio.* DAVE *turns to* JOE.) How was that, Joe? Do you think I'm holding my own against Renfrew of the Mounted?

JOE

I think you're wasting your breath, Dave. Nobody's listening.

GUS

I don't see how they can—with the complicated hook-up we've got now. And if one of those bombs today had landed fifty yards farther west, there wouldn't be any broadcasting station here at all. Did you see those craters?

DAVE

Yes.

GUS

Boy! They must be dropping those two-ton bombs now, like they had in Spain.

DAVE

Are you going to be flying around here now to protect us, Joe?

JOE

I doubt it. I guess I'll get shipped right back to the lines.

GUS

Well, I hope they don't keep us here until it's too late to get out. I'd hate to go through Warsaw again. I think I'll go down and see if I can get a cup of coffee. Where's the sugar?

DAVE

Here. (*He hands* GUS *an envelope filled with sugar that has been lying on the couch.*)

GUS (*to* JOE)

See you later.

JOE

Sure.

(GUS *goes out.*)

Say, Dave—when you were in Viipuri, did you see anything of Ben and Frank and Dr. Valkonen?

DAVE

Yes. They got their hospitals established there and now they're working day and night to evacuate them. Ben and Frank don't seem to be having a very good time in this war.

JOE

I guess they're in a tough spot now, with those attacks across Viipuri Bay.

DAVE

Yes, I've got to go and see Mrs. Valkonen and try to think of something encouraging to say. Last week I was up in the north. I saw some of the ski troops in action.

JOE

Did you see Mrs. Valkonen's son?

DAVE

No. But I got an idea of what he must be going through. Poor kid. I remember the first time I came here he said that Finland wouldn't. be in danger unless there was a counter-revolution in Russia. He had that much faith in them. Well—it seems that the counter-revolution has come.

JOE

Something else has come. I saw something to-day that might interest you.

DAVE

What was it?

JOE

Maybe I oughtn't to be talking to the press.

DAVE

Now listen, Joe—have another drink.

JOE

Thanks. (*He pours himself another drink.*)

DAVE

You understand, Joe. Anything you tell me will be considered strictly confidential. I'll only try to pass it on the A.P., the U.P. and the radio audience. But the censorship will stop me, so your secrets will be sacred.

(JOE *drinks.*)

JOE

Well, they sent me·out reconnoitering. I wanted to know what was the greatest point of Russian concentration. I had to fly very low. The weather was closing in and the ceiling was only seven or eight hundred feet, when I was coming back. I couldn't find the field I took off from. That's why I had to fly back here to make my report to the war office.

DAVE

What did you report, Joe?

JOE

I saw some staff cars coming up to the town that seemed to be general headquarters. I didn't know the name of the town, but I identified it for them on the map. I dived to give those cars a few bursts. They were full of staff officers, all right. But they weren't Russians. They were Nazis. It gave me a thrill. All this time, in fighting the Russians, I've felt just a little bit uncomfortable—you can im-

agine it, Dave, after my experience with the Loyalists. You know, I couldn't help saying, "God forgive them—for they know not what they do." If
that's the right quotation.

DAVE

It's good enough.

JOE

But when I saw those Nazis—those arrogant
bastards—and I could even see the looks on their
faces—all I could think of was, "God forgive *me* if
I miss this glorious opportunity." I let 'em have
it. It was a beautiful sight to see 'em diving into
the ditches, mussing their slick gray uniforms in
the mud.

DAVE

Did you get any of them?

JOE

I'm afraid I'll never know. It was just then that
the Russian planes came up. And I had to take
my ship away from there.

DAVE

I thought it was about time for the Nazis to be
taking a hand in this war. No wonder the tide of
battle has turned. I guess they've decided there
has been enough of this nonsense of Finland's resistance. Probably they want the Russians to get
busy somewhere else.

(JOE *puts his glass down and stands up.*)

JOE

Is there any news from home?

DAVE

Yes. . . . This has been the biggest season in the history of Miami Beach. The University of Southern California won the national basketball championship. The Beaux Arts Ball was an outstanding success.

(JOE *crosses and looks into the bedroom at the left.*)

JOE

Good! Say, Dave—can I have the use of that elegant bathtub of yours?

DAVE

Certainly. There may be some hot water, and maybe not.

JOE

How are you fixed for a clean shirt and underwear and socks? (JOE *goes into the bedroom.*)

DAVE

I guess Gus and I can fit you out between us.

(DAVE *follows* JOE *out. There is a knock at the door at the right.*)

Come in!

(MIRANDA *comes in. Her face is pale. She comes in quietly, closing the door behind her.* DAVE *calls from off left.*)

I'll be right out.

(MIRANDA *looks around the room, then sits*

down. After a moment DAVE *comes back, and is
startled to see her.*)

Mrs. Valkonen! (*He closes the bedroom door behind him.*)

MIRANDA

Hello, Dave. I hope I'm not disturbing you.
Mr. Shuman told me I might come up—I met him
in the lobby.

DAVE

Of course, Mrs. Valkonen. I apologize for the
mess here. . . . Would you like anything to drink?

MIRANDA

No, thank you. I came to ask you for some
help, Dave.

DAVE

Anything that I can do——

MIRANDA

I want to get my daughter-in-law out of this
country.

DAVE

Your daughter-in-law? ˙(*He sits down, near
her.*)

MIRANDA

Yes. You've met her—Kaatri. She was married
a few days ago to my son, Erik. They were married in the hospital, before he died.

DAVE

Oh—I'm terribly sorry.

MIRANDA

I know you're sorry, Dave. . . . Kaatri is going to have a baby. . . . She's very ill. I've made
all the arrangements to get her to Norway, and
then to New York. But she has to leave right
away. I need some American money, Dave. Could
you lend me fifty dollars? It will be paid back.

DAVE

Will that be enough?

MIRANDA

Oh, yes—that will be plenty. And— (*She opens
her handbag and takes out a sheet of paper.*) —
here is the name and address of my aunt in Boston.
When you get back to America, just write to her
and tell her where to send the money.
(DAVE *takes the paper and puts it down on the
table. He takes out his wallet.*)
You see—the Finnish money is worth very little in
foreign exchange now. By the time Kaatri arrives
in New York, it might be completely worthless.
That's why I had to have dollars. If it's incon-
venient for you—I'm sure I can get it somewhere
else—so please don't hesitate to——

DAVE

It's perfectly convenient, and I'm very much
flattered that you came to me. (*He gives her the
fifty dollars.*)

MIRANDA

Thank you. We had an awful time persuading
Kaatri to go. We never could have persuaded her
if she weren't too ill to resist. She's strong—but
there are limits. (*She puts the money in her handbag.*)

DAVE

I wish you were going with her.

MIRANDA

I wish I could. I should like to be present at the
birth of my grandchild. Poor Kaatri. She'll have
a bad time of it, all alone there. . . . Perhaps
she'll have a son, and he'll grow up a nice, respecta-
ble New Englander and go to Harvard and wonder
why he has an odd name like Valkonen. . . . Erik
wasn't very badly wounded. He might have pulled
through if he hadn't been in such a state of terrible
exhaustion. It was a lucky thing that we learned
where he was and got to him. I sent word to Kaarlo. I don't know where he is—somewhere around
Viipuri. (*She looks at* DAVE.) They're getting
closer, aren't they, Dave?

DAVE

Yes.
(MIRANDA *rises.*)

MIRANDA

I'm very grateful for that loan. I hope you will
come to see Uncle Waldemar and me. We're always there.

DAVE

Thank you, Mrs. Valkonen. I—I wish to God you'd let me really *do* something.

MIRANDA

But you've done a lot, Dave. That fifty dollars——

DAVE

It's not much satisfaction to know that fifty dollars is the best I can do.

MIRANDA

It's all I want, Dave. All I can use. I was desperately anxious to get Kaatri out of the country. You can understand why. It means one little link with the future. It gives us the illusion of survival—and perhaps it isn't just an illusion. . . . Good-bye, Dave.

DAVE

Good-bye.

(MIRANDA *goes out*.)

CURTAIN

SCENE VI

Classroom in a little country schoolhouse in eastern Finland. It is afternoon of a gloomy day, a few days after the preceding scene.

This schoolhouse is new and clean, designed in the most modern style. Huge, opaque glass windows would admit plenty of soft sunshine if there were any today.

At the center upstage is a dais. Before it is a row of pupil's desks. The size of these desks indicates that this is a classroom for little children of nine or ten. There is a blackboard with arithmetical problems. On the walls are tacked rows of sketches done by the pupils. Around the room on the walls are painted, in decorative, colored Finnish script, the first ten lines of the "Kalevala." (Of course, half of these lines are on the walls which we do not see.) On the window sills, little plants are sprouting in pots.

There is a door at the extreme left, leading to the little enclosed porch, and a door at the extreme right, leading to another schoolroom.

At one of the pupils' desks, the right one, Gos-
DEN *is sitting solemnly playing solitaire with an old, dirty pack. He is a mild, tired Englishman, about forty years old. He wears the uniform of an infantry soldier. His rifle lies on the desk be-*

fore him. There is a scuffle at the door, left.
GOSDEN *leaps to his feet, picks up his rifle and aims it at the door.* BEN GICHNER *and* FRANK OLMSTEAD *come in. Both carry large haversacks. Both are very cold.*

GOSDEN

Who are you?
(BEN *and* FRANK *raise their arms immediately.*)

BEN

Friends! We're not Russians and we're not armed.

GOSDEN (*lowering his rifle*)

Glad to see you. Sorry but I'm a bit jumpy these days.

BEN

That's all right, pal.

GOSDEN

Americans, eh!

BEN

That's right. What are you—English?

GOSDEN

Yes. The name is Gosden. I don't rightly know what my rank is in this army, but I call myself "Sergeant."

BEN (*crossing and shaking hands with* GOSDEN)

Glad to know you, Sergeant. My name is Ben Gichner—this is Frank Olmstead.

FRANK

Glad to know you. (FRANK *sits at the desk at the left.*)

GOSDEN

Thank you. It's a pleasure to have your company. I was getting the wind up, all alone here. (*Sees their uniforms.*) You chaps in the Medical Corps?

BEN

Yes. Ambulance drivers. Only—we've lost our ambulance—it's frozen stiff as a goat in a snowdrift. When the Russians occupy this territory they'll come into possession of a Buick.

GOSDEN

You wouldn't have much use for it here. There haven't been many wounded since we retreated from the Mannerheim Line. Only dead and missing.

(FRANK *rests his head on his arms.*)

FRANK

How far are the Russians from here?

GOSDEN

I wish I knew. They've probably occupied those islands out there in Viipuri Bay. Maybe they've already reached this shore. All I can say is the last time I saw them they were coming in this direction, driving us across the ice. I've been retreating across the ice for days. I've felt like a bloody Eskimo. (*He looks about the room.*) Nice little schoolhouse, this. (*He reaches in his pocket.*) Like a bit of chocolate?

FRANK

No, thanks.

BEN (*sitting up*)

I'll have some.

GOSDEN (*tossing him some candy*)

It's good for energy.

BEN

Thanks, pal.

FRANK

How long have you been in this war?

GOSDEN

I joined up in London, just after Christmas.

FRANK

Why? What did you want to come here for?

GOSDEN (*smiles*)

Are you trying to trap me into making any remarks about fighting for freedom and democracy?

FRANK (*wearily*)

No.

GOSDEN

Because I had enough of *that* muck when I fought in the last war!

FRANK

I'm just interested to know why *any*body vol-
unteered.

GOSDEN

Well, you might say that my case is no different
from any of the others. I came because I was
bored, fed up. My wife and two little children were
sent to Cornwall in the evacuation. Then I lost my
job. I was working in the furniture department at
Harrod's—and who wants to buy furniture in war
time? I couldn't join up with our own army—too
old. All I could do was walk the streets looking at
nothing. There was no news to read in the papers
—except about heroic little Finland. On Christmas,
I felt I couldn't stick it out any longer. So—I
thought—why not have a go at heroic little Finland? And here I am. Where I shall be tomorrow,
I really couldn't say.

(RUTKOWSKI *comes in from the left, followed by*
KAARLO, *who wears a Red Cross arm band on his
uniform. All the men rise to attention.*)

RUTKOWSKI

At ease! Are there any more men here?

GOSDEN

No, sir. Only me. I was with Captain Vertti's
company, but we got separated. I didn't know
just where to go next, sir, so I stopped here for a
bit of a rest.

RUTKOWSKI

Has there been much shelling here?

GOSDEN

I've heard plenty of heavies, overhead, but none dropping here, sir. There's also been a lot of Bolshie planes, flying low—looking the situation over, I expect.

RUTKOWSKI

They're probably shelling the railroad line between Viipuri and Helsinki. Trying to cut off all possibilities of re-enforcement. I'm going out to find if there is any one in command here.

(KAARLO *is greatly interested in the school-room. He crosses to the right.*)

KAARLO

This schoolhouse would do well for a field ambulance station.

(BEN *and* FRANK *have sat down.*)

GOSDEN (*still standing*)

Begging your pardon, sir. You couldn't find a more exposed place.

RUTKOWSKI

Yes—you might say that this *is* Finland—small —clean—and exposed. (*With a slight shrug.*) I shall be back presently, Doctor. (*He goes out at the left.*)

KAARLO

We'll be waiting, Major. (*To* GOSDEN.) I'm Dr. Valkonen. How do you do?

(*Somewhat to* GOSDEN's *surprise,* KAARLO *extends his hand. They shake.*)

GOSDEN

Thank you, sir. My name is Gosden.

KAARLO

I gather that things here are a bit disorganized.

GOSDEN

And no wonder, sir. It's a miracle that there's any sign of an army left—the way they've been pushing us.

(GOSDEN *sits.* KAARLO *crosses to the dais and looks at the blackboard.*)

KAARLO

You know—they must have left this school very quickly—right in the midst of an arithmetic lesson. Look—there's a multiplication problem that was never finished. The pupils were probably delighted but— (*pointing to the sketches*) —they evidently had to leave without knowing which picture won first prize.

BEN

How old would the kids be in a school like this?

KAARLO

From seven to twelve I should judge. It's just a little country school. I wish you could see it when the children are here. The boys are on that side, the girls there. When the teacher comes in,

the boys all rise and bow stiffly. The girls make
their little curtsys. Maybe in their hearts they
loathe the teacher—but they're always very polite.
And all very full of moral preachments. Oh, yes.
. . . You see that inscription all around the walls?
That's from the Kalevala—the epic poem of Finland. It had its beginnings in the songs of our
minstrels a thousand years ago. Your poet, Long-
fellow, knew the Kalevala and used its rhythm in
Hiawatha. (*He looks up, and starts to recite, at
first with a sort of tender amusement, and then
with increasing solemnity. His eyes travel about
the room as he follows the inscription.*)
> "Let us clasp our hands together,
>   Let us interlock our fingers;
>   Let us sing a cheerful measure,
>   Let us use our best endeavors
>   While our dear ones hearken to us,
>   And our loved ones are instructed,
>   While the young are standing round us,
>   Of the rising generation,
>   Let them learn the words of magic,
>   And recall our songs and legends."

(*He is quiet for a moment, looking toward the
right. Then he turns to the others.*)
Every Finnish child learns about the Kalevala—
just as Americans learn those words about Life,
Liberty and the Pursuit of Happiness.

FRANK (*earnestly*)

Dr. Valkonen——

KAARLO

Yes, Frank?

FRANK

I've wanted to ask you a question——

KAARLO

Yes?

FRANK

About your book— (FRANK *pulls a paper-cov-ered book, badly dog-eared, from his jacket pocket.*)

KAARLO

You've been carrying that around with you?

FRANK

Yes. I bought it in Viipuri when we first went there.

BEN

Frank is more worried about your book, Doctor, than he is about the Russians.

FRANK (*he opens the book to the last page*)

There's a lot of it I don't understand, but what I wanted to ask you about most is the very end.

KAARLO

What is it at the end?

FRANK (*reads*)

"How long, O Lord, before we shall hear the sound of the Seventh Angel of the Apocalypse? Have you forgotten the promise of St. John? 'And they shall see his face, and his name shall be in their foreheads. And there shall be no night there and they need no candle, neither light of the sun; for the Lord giveth them light; and they shall reign forever and ever.' How long, O Lord, before we shall be given to see the true revelation?" (FRANK *closes the book and looks at* KAARLO.) Why did you conclude a scientific work with Biblical words—and what do you mean by the true revelation?

KAARLO (*simply*)

It's the revealing to us of ourselves—of what we are—and what we may be. (*Smiles.*) Of course—we can all use the Book of Revelation to substantiate our own theories. It's an eternally effective device. I have heard evangelist charlatans quote it to prove that if you do not accept their nonsense and pay for it, you will most surely burn in hell. But there is something profound in those words I quoted. That unknown Jewish mystic who wrote that—somehow, unconsciously, he knew that man will find the true name of God in his own forehead, in the mysteries of his own mind. "And there shall be no night there." That is the basis of all the work I have done.

FRANK

And how do you feel about that work now, Dr. Valkonen?

KAARLO

I think I've learned a great deal in the last few months. Research work in the field! I never dreamed I would have such a vast laboratory, with so many specimens.

BEN

Have you arrived at any new conclusions, Doctor?

KAARLO

Not conclusions, I'm afraid. Just—somewhat stronger suspicions. It is wonderful to see what men are capable of—what courage—what endurance—what utter lack of selfishness. And what a tragedy that these heroic qualities can be tested only by disease. That's what all this is, you know —disease. All of this—reasonless war—aimless revolution—it's a psychological epidemic. (*He rises. It is as though he were lecturing to a class.*) Scientists had seen it coming, for a long time, long before 1914, even. But we had no conception of its extent. And now the very belief of men that they can insulate themselves against it is in itself a sign of lunacy. The germs of that disease travel on the air waves. The only defenses are still here— behind the forehead. . . . (*He pauses and smiles, looking particularly at* GOSDEN.) I apologize, gentlemen, for carrying on a conversation which must be extremely boring to you.

GOSDEN

I'm an ignorant man, sir. I haven't read this book. I didn't even know I was in the presence of any one who had written a book. But—from what you've said—I have a feeling it's all hopeless. I shouldn't care to die believing *that*.

KAARLO

Then you won't die believing it's hopeless. That's the point, my friend. You have lived in faith—the light is in you—and it is the light which gives the strength that defeats death. It's only the fearful—the unbelieving—those who have sold themselves to the murderers and the liars—they are the only ones who can really die.

FRANK

But how can you deny that the light is going out —it's going fast—everywhere?

KAARLO (*with a growing sense of excitement*)

It is just beginning to burn with a healthy flame. I know this, because I have seen it. I have seen it in all kinds of men, of all races, and all varieties of faith. They are coming to consciousness. Look at all the millions of men now under arms, and all those that are fearful that arms may be thrust upon them. Are there any illusions of glory among any of them? None whatever! Isn't that progress?

BEN

Far be it from me to argue, Doctor—but I can't see the difference whether men go to war because of illusions of glory, or just in a spirit of grim resignation.

KAARLO

There is all the difference. Because those illusions, when shattered, leave men hollow. When men lose their illusions, they say, "Oh, what's the use? What have we got to live for?" They are devitalized by the conviction of futility. But grim resignation, as you call it, that makes a man say, "This is an evil job—but I have to do it." And when men say that, they are already beginning to ask, "But *why* do I have to do it? *Why* must this evil go on forever?" And when men start asking questions, they are not satisfied until they find the answers. That is consciousness. And for the first time in history, consciousness is not just the privilege of a few secluded philosophers. It is free for all. For the first time, individual men are fighting to know themselves. . . . Forgive me, gentlemen. I forget myself. I think I am lecturing at the Medical Institute. But— (*He pauses to listen to the guns*) —the Russians are only a short distance away. This may be my last lecture. So—please permit me to finish. . . . Listen! What you hear now— this terrible sound that fills the earth—it is the death rattle. One may say easily and dramatically that it is the death rattle of civilization. But—I choose to believe differently. I believe it is the long deferred death rattle of the primordial beast. We have within ourselves the power to conquer bestiality, not with our muscles and our swords, but with the power of the light that is in our minds. What a thrilling challenge this is to all Science! To play its part in the ultimate triumph of evolution. To help speed the day when man becomes genuinely human, instead of the synthetic creature—part bogus angel, part actual brute—that he has imagined himself in the dark past——

(*The sound of an approaching motorcycle is heard.*)

Is that an aeroplane?

(*All the men listen, tensely.*)

GOSDEN

No. It's a motorbike.

(*The sound stops.*)

Just a despatch rider, I expect. Maybe it's orders.

(JOE BURNETT *comes in from the left.*)

JOE

Hello, Ben. Hello, Frank. Hello, Doctor Valkonen.

FRANK

Joe!

BEN

Where did *you* drop from?

JOE

I saw Major Rutkowski up the road. He said you were in here.

KAARLO

Mr. Burnett! I am delighted to see you. Are you flying on this front now?

JOE

I was—up till half an hour ago. I was shot down.
First time that ever happened to me. I just man-
aged to make a landing behind our lines. I got a
motor-cycle and I'm going back to headquarters to
see if they have any more planes.

GOSDEN

Were you scouting the Russian lines?

JOE

Yes.

GOSDEN

How do things look?

JOE

Not too good. They're bringing up everything.

BEN

Have you been in Helsinki lately, Joe?

JOE

Yes. I was there a few days ago.

BEN

Is Dave Corween still on the job?

JOE

Yes. He's still telling bed-time stories.

KAARLO

And I hope you called at my house, Mr. Burnett?
Did you see my wife?

JOE

No—I didn't. (*He braces himself and crosses to* KAARLO.) I—I don't know how to say it, Doctor Valkonen—although God knows I've said it so many times before—but—I want you to know that you have my sympathy.

KAARLO

Your sympathy? (KAARLO *looks at him with such intense questioning that* JOE *gulps.*) Why do I have your sympathy, Mr. Burnett?

JOE

You don't know about your son?

KAARLO

No. (*He looks levelly at* JOE.) He's dead?

JOE

Yes.

KAARLO

Killed in action?

JOE

I believe he died in hospital, of wounds.

KAARLO

When was this?

JOE

I don't quite know. I heard of it only from Dave. He had seen Mrs. Valkonen.

KAARLO

Is—my wife well?

JOE

Yes, Doctor. She told Dave that she had been with your son in the hospital. He was married there, to Miss Alquist, before he died. His wife has gone to America. . . . I—I didn't know, Doctor, that I should be the bearer of this news— (*His voice trails off.*)

GOSDEN (*rising, and speaking with great diffidence.*)

I should like, sir, to be permitted to put in my word of sympathy, too.

BEN

And mine also, Doctor.

FRANK (*rising*)

Wouldn't you like us to get out of here, Doctor Valkonen?

KAARLO

No, no. Thank you. And thank you for telling me, Mr. Burnett. I imagine my wife has written me all this, but we have moved about so much that there have been no letters in weeks. I'm sorry you had to undergo this embarrassment.

(RUTKOWSKI *comes in. He carries a cartridge belt with a revolver in a holster.*)

RUTKOWSKI

I found the commanding officer. The Russians have occupied all the islands around Uuras. They're bringing tanks over the ice, and they're

going to attack in force here. The Finns are forming up to drive them back. They need more men.
They seem to be organizing the defense very well.
But they have no reserves. They need more men.
There's no point in trying to organize a field
ambulance station here, Doctor. I brought this
revolver and belt for you. It was salvaged from
some officer who was killed. There are rifles for
you men to use.

(*He hands the belt and holster to* KAARLO,
who takes out the revolver and stares at it.)

FRANK

We're to fight?

RUTKOWSKI

There's no compulsion if you don't wish to go.

JOE (*quietly*)

I'll be glad to go, Major.

BEN

So will I.

RUTKOWSKI (*to* JOE)

Not you, Lieutenant. If there are any planes
left, we need them in the air. You will report back
to headquarters at Sakkijaarvi.

JOE (*resigned*)

Very good, sir.

KAARLO

We must go now? At once?

RUTKOWSKI

We may as well wait here for a little while. There will be plenty of warning when the attack starts.

KAARLO

Then—I would like to write a letter. (*He puts the revolver and belt down on the desk.*) Perhaps you will take it with you, Mr. Burnett? There must be some way that they could send it on to Helsinki.

JOE

I'll do everything I possibly can, Doctor Valkonen.

KAARLO (*to* RUTKOWSKI)

If I'm not finished when you're ready to go, just call me.

RUTKOWSKI

I will, Doctor.

(KAARLO *goes out at the right, taking his fountain pen from his pocket.*)

Have any of you gentlemen a cigarette?

(BEN *hands him one.*)

Thank you. . . . I suppose Doctor Valkonen wants to write his valedictory.

JOE

It isn't that, Major. I just gave him the news that his son was killed.

RUTKOWSKI

Oh—when I came in—I saw his face—but I didn't know the explanation. (*He lights his cigarette,*

being careful to mask the flame with his great-
coat.)

FRANK (*with sudden vehemence*)

Do you know that Doctor Valkonen believes in
the teachings of Christ? He believes in them as if
they were scientific facts, which can yet be proved.
He says so in his book. He says you can't resist
evil by building Maginot Lines and big navies.
The true defenses of man are *in* man, himself. . . .
So now—there's nothing left for that great thinker
to do but take a gun and go up there and shoot.
(*He has crossed above the desks and looks at the
revolver.*)

BEN

And how about you, Frank? Are you going up?
What does the old conscience say?

FRANK

What the hell do you think it says? How could
I ever live with myself again if I didn't go? That's
what happens when you expose yourself to this.
Oh, God—how many times have I taken an oath
that if the United States were ever again duped
into going to war, I'll be a conscientious objector!
Let them put me in Leavenworth. I'd rather be
there. I'd consider it takes more courage to be
there than in the front line. But—here's the choice
—given to me now—and I haven't got the guts to
say, "No—I won't fight."

(*He has crossed to the left and sits down on the
floor beside* JOE. RUTKOWSKI *is sitting on the cen-*

*ter desk. The others are seated at the other
desks.)*

BEN

Why don't you put all that into a poem, Frank?

FRANK

All right, Ben—go ahead and kid me.

BEN

I don't feel in a position to kid you, Frank.
I've had a few necessary changes of heart myself.
Once I lost a good job because they decided I was
a Red. Yes. I've spent hours arguing that the
Soviet Union is the greatest sociological advance
in history—the greatest force for peace on earth
today. . . . Now—go ahead and kid *me!*

RUTKOWSKI (*bitterly*)

Nobody is responsible for his opinions now.
There *are* no opinions on anything.

GOSDEN (*to* RUTKOWSKI)

How do our positions look in the line, sir?

RUTKOWSKI

Fairly well placed.

GOSDEN

Do you think we would have any chance of
holding them?

RUTKOWSKI (*with no emotion*)

No—I don't think so.

BEN (*with a nervous laugh*)

I take it, Major—you feel we're all condemned to death?

RUTKOWSKI

Yes.

(BEN *stands up. He is whistling.*)

BEN

I can't help agreeing with you, Frank. It seems a silly way to end your life.

JOE

Any way is silly. A cousin of mine was killed—he and his girl both—driving home from a debutante party at the Ritz in New York. He was a little tight, and he didn't notice the Dead End sign —and—phft!—right into the East River!

FRANK

And is that any reason why we should fight—and die?

GOSDEN (*to* FRANK)

Every one of us can find plenty of reasons for *not* fighting, and they're the best reasons in the world. But—the time comes when you've bloody well got to fight—and you might just as well go cheerfully.

FRANK (*rising to his knees*)

Cheerful! What are you, anyway? Are you so stupid you can't even *think?* You said you have a wife and two little children in England. Aren't you giving any thought to them now?

GOSDEN (*in a choked voice*)

I'll have to ask you not to mention them. My people know what I'm doing—and why.

FRANK (*sinking back on his heels*)

Excuse me.

RUTKOWSKI (*looking off toward the left*)

Poor Doctor Valkonen. He is a philosopher. He is also, for some strange reason, an optimist. He will be better dead.

BEN

Why do you say that, Major?

RUTKOWSKI

Perhaps it is only because I am Polish. (*He looks levelly at* FRANK.) You asked this gentleman to give a thought to his wife and children in England. He can think of them happily. My wife—my baby —my father—and mother—are in Warsaw—or they were there, when the Nazis came. My wife is twenty-four years old. She is very beautiful. She is the most beautiful person I have ever known. And I have read in Cardinal Hlond's report, that he has sent to the Pope—I have read that the good-looking women and the girls in Poland have been sent into Germany to be whores. (*He rises quickly and raps at the door at the right. He turns to the others.*) Well!

GOSDEN (*in a desperate effort to change the subject*)

I wish I'd thought to write a line myself. I *did* think of it—but I didn't know what to say. I wish I'd written to my missus to tell her I'm going up the line in good company.

(KAARLO *comes in from the right. He is sealing the envelope.* BEN *slaps* GOSDEN *on the back.*)

KAARLO

Here you are, Mr. Burnett.

(JOE *crosses and gets the letter from* KAARLO.)

JOE

I'm sure it will be delivered safely.

(*He shakes hands with* KAARLO, *and salutes* RUTKOWSKI, *who returns the salute.*)

KAARLO

.Thank you so much.

JOE

Good-bye, sir.

(GOSDEN *picks up his coat and rifle. All are now making preparations to go.* KAARLO *goes to the desk to get the belt and revolver and put them on.*)

GOSDEN (*to* JOE)

Best of luck, mate.

JOE

Same to you.

(GOSDEN *goes out.* JOE *is about to go.*)

BEN

Joe, if you ever get back, I wish you'd send a word to my mother, Mrs. Bessie Gichner—Cincinnati. You can get her address at the American Express Company's main office in New York. They all know me there.

JOE (*as* BEN *goes out*)

I'll remember that, Ben . . . (*He starts out.*) If I get back——

FRANK

Hey, Joe—wait a minute. I've got a message, too!

(JOE *and* FRANK *have gone out on this.* RUTKOWSKI *has been watching* KAARLO *with silent sympathy as he puts on the belt.*)

RUTKOWSKI

Forgive me, Doctor Valkonen. I hadn't known of the great loss you have suffered.

KAARLO

Thank you. I had been expecting that news for a long time. I was prepared for it. My son had a good character—part Finnish, part American. He was not afraid.

(*He starts to go.* RUTKOWSKI *is by the door at the left.*)

RUTKOWSKI

Doctor, I think you had better take off that Red Cross arm band.

(RUTKOWSKI *goes. It is now so dark that* KAARLO *is a silhouette as he rips off the Red Cross arm band. He goes out. The sound of the guns increases.*)

CURTAIN

SCENE VII

*The Valkonens' living room. The only no-
ticeable difference in the room is that all the auto-
graphed photographs have been removed from
their frames.*

*Uncle Waldemar is at a window, looking out.
It is a beautiful, sunny day.*

*After a moment, Dave and Joe come in from
the dining room. Uncle Waldemar turns
quickly.*

Uncle Waldemar

I was enjoying the beautiful day.

Dave

It *is* beautiful. It's beginning to feel almost
like spring.

Uncle Waldemar

Did you have a nice lunch?

Dave

Wonderful, thank you.

Uncle Waldemar

I'll go help Miranda clear the dishes.

Dave

We begged to be allowed to help, but were ordered out of the kitchen.

UNCLE WALDEMAR

Of course. (*He gives them a courtly bow.*) You are guests.

(*He goes out.* DAVE *offers* JOE *a cigarette.*)

DAVE

An incredible display of stoicism.

JOE

God—I didn't know what to say. I never know what to say. Anything you can think of sounds so lame.

DAVE

You didn't need to say anything, Joe. She's lost everybody that she loves—and now she's in terrible danger of losing her own life. But it's a matter of principle that neither she nor any one else must ever admit that there are certain undertones of tragedy in the situation. After all the centuries, New England is still New England. You might even go so far as to say that it's still England. Keeping a stiff upper lip.

JOE

How long do you figure it will take the Russians to get here?

DAVE

I don't know. But I suspect it won't be long. Berlin has given out orders that this little incident must end—and if the Russians don't hurry, there are going to be some serious tantrums in the Wilhelmstrasse.

JOE

This city might hold out for a long time, like Madrid.

DAVE

I hope not. Because if it comes to a siege, you'll see German battleships out there, doing their bit in the bombardment. I wouldn't like to be here when that happens. I saw them at Danzig when they were battering Westerplatte. I could see the Nazis, watching their own barrage. They were deriving a sexual thrill from thát display of devastating power.

JOE

What happens to you when you get caught in a captured city?

DAVE

I know how to wave my little red passport. I can say "I'm an American journalist" in all languages. In Nanking, I had to say it in Japanese. Oh—I get pushed around a bit—but I always live to broadcast the final hours of another gallant little republic. . . . But what about you, Joe? Have you got a plane?

JOE

I don't know. I may be in the army now. It would be pretty humiliating to end my career in the god-damned infantry.

DAVE (*looking toward the kitchen*)
That's what Doctor Valkonen did.
(JOE *also glances toward the kitchen.*)

JOE

Listen, Dave—can't you get Mrs. Valkonen out of this—and the old man, too?

DAVE

I've tried—but they won't leave. They're going to wait here for whatever comes, the Russians, or the Nazis, or both. They've even planned how they'll burn the house down. That's required by Finnish tradition. It's like the scorched earth in China. Mrs. Valkonen wants to stay here and die, just as her husband did. She doesn't care what happens.

JOE

It's a pity.

DAVE

That's just what it is, Joe. A wholesale pity. Three months ago, the Soviet troops marched in. They had brass bands and truck-loads of propaganda with them. They thought it would be a grand parade through Finland, like May Day in the Red Square. So now—several hundred thousand men have been killed—millions of lives have been ruined. The cause of revolution all over the world has been set back incalculably. The Soviet Union has been reduced from the status of a great power to that of a great fraud. And the Nazis have won another bloodless victory.

(MIRANDA *and* UNCLE WALDEMAR *come in from the kitchen.* MIRANDA *wears an apron, but her*

dress is, as always, very feminine and chic. DAVE
and JOE *rise.*)

MIRANDA

Well—we've washed all the dishes and put them
away neatly, and now Uncle Waldemar and I
haven't a thing to do until supper. Sit down,
Dave—Mr. Burnett.

JOE

I'm sorry, Mrs. Valkonen. I have to go and
report for duty, whatever it is.

MIRANDA

Oh—I'm sorry. But thank you so much for coming, and bringing the letter, and telling me all
about that little schoolhouse.

JOE

I—I'm glad I could get here. You've been very
kind to me. I can tell you that—I won't ever forget you, or Doctor Valkonen. . . . Good-bye, Mr.
Sederstrum. (*He shakes hands with* UNCLE
WALDEMAR.) Good-bye, Dave—I'll probably be
seeing you. (*He shakes hands with* DAVE.)

DAVE

Yes, Joe—good-bye.

JOE

And if you get home before I do, don't forget
those messages for Ben's and Frank's families.

DAVE

I won't, Joe.

MIRANDA

I wish you the very best of luck, Mr. Burnett.

JOE

You needn't worry about me, Mrs. Valkonen. The beautiful part of my life is that it's so utterly worthless nobody bothers to deprive me of it. Good-bye. (*He goes out at the right.*)

MIRANDA

I hope he comes through all right. He's the only one left of those young men who went to Viipuri with Kaarlo . . . I suppose you'll be going soon, Dave?

DAVE

I'm not sure, Mrs. Valkonen. There's some talk of their sending me to Stockholm. They want to investigate those peace rumors.

MIRANDA

Do you think there might be peace before the Russians get here to Helsinki?

DAVE

I hope so.

UNCLE WALDEMAR (*in a completely matter-of-fact tone*)
It doesn't make much difference. Either the war continues and we suffer the fate of Poland, or peace comes, as it did at Munich, and we become

another Czechoslovakia. In any case, we live only at the mercy of the enemy.

MIRANDA

You'll have a great book to write about all this —won't you, Dave? Your own personal history.

DAVE

I'm afraid that words will fail me, Mrs. Valkonen. Just as they've failed the whole human race.

MIRANDA

I'd like to read your book, Dave.

DAVE (*he looks at her*)

What are you going to do, Mrs. Valkonen? Are you—are you planning just to sit here and wait for them?

MIRANDA

Oh no, we have our plans all made. Get out the guns, Uncle Waldemar.

(UNCLE WALDEMAR *goes out at the right.*)

DAVE

Guns?

MIRANDA

We got them at the hospital. They'd been discarded by wounded soldiers. Uncle Waldemar and I have been practicing—not shooting, of course; but just learning how to work them. When this war started, Dave—when the Russians first

attacked us—the President said we would fight—
even the women, and the old people, and the children would fight. We have no children here—only
that one in Boston, who is unborn. But Uncle
Waldemar and I are here.

(UNCLE WALDEMAR *returns with two army
rifles and some cartridge belts.*)

When we see them coming from the shore down
there, we'll light the fire. It's all ready, down in
the cellar. Then we'll go out into the garden, behind the stone wall, with the guns and ammunition.
(*She takes one of the rifles and a clip of ammunition.*) You see—you put the clip in like this—
then you shove the bolt. (*She shoves it with a
snap.*) After each shot, you twist it and pull it
back, to throw out the empty shell. Like this . . .
(*She demonstrates, manipulating the bolt. The
shells fly out.*) What do you think of that, Dave?
(*She looks up at the 1812 portrait.*) Great-
grandfather Eustis thinks it's fine!

(*There is something maniacal in this statement.
She puts the gun against the wall and picks up a
parcel from the piano.*)

I hate to add to your burdens as a carrier of bad
news, Dave. But—I have a package here, that I
want you to take, and also a letter from Kaarlo—
the one he wrote in the schoolhouse before he was
killed. The package contains Kaarlo's signed pictures of Freud and Pavlov and Carrel and the
Mayos. He was very proud of those pictures.

There's also the Nobel gold medal. I want you to take the package and the letter and give them to Kaatri, to keep for her child. You have that address in Boston—my aunt, who is going to pay you back the fifty dollars I borrowed?

DAVE

Yes. I have the address.

MIRANDA (*looking at the letter*)

Kaarlo had just heard from me about Erik's death. He wanted to comfort me, in his curious way. Do you mind if I read you the letter?

DAVE

Please do, Mrs. Valkonen.

MIRANDA (*reading*)

"In this time of our own grief it is not easy to summon up the philosophy which has been formed from long study of the sufferings of others. But I must do it, and you must help me." You see—he wanted to make me feel that I'm stronger—wiser. "I hÅve often read the words which Pericles spoke over the bodies of the dead, in the dark hour when the light of Athenian democracy was being extinguished by the Spartans. He told the mourning people that he could not give them any of the old words which tell how fair and noble it is to die in battle. Those empty words were old, even then, twenty-four centuries ago. But he urged them to find revival in the memory of the commonwealth which they together had achieved; and he promised them that the story of their commonwealth would never die, but would live on, far away, woven into the fabric of other men's lives. I believe that these words can be said now of our own dead, and our own commonwealth. I have always believed in the mystic truth of the resurrection. The great leaders of the mind and the spirit—Socrates, Christ, Lincoln—were all done to death that the full measure of their contribution to human experience might never be lost. Now—the death of our son is only a fragment in the death of our country. But Erik and the others who give their lives are also giving to mankind a symbol—a little symbol, to be sure, but a clear one—of man's unconquerable aspiration to dignity and freedom and purity in the sight of God. When I made that radio speech" —you remember? . . . "I quoted from St. Paul. I repeat those words to you now, darling: 'We glory in tribulations; knowing that tribulation worketh patience; and patience, experience; and experience, hope.' There are men here from all different countries. Fine men. Those Americans who were at our house on New Year's Day—and that nice Polish officer, Major Rutkowski—they are all here. They are waiting for me now, so I must close this, with all my love."

(*She folds the letter and hands it to* Dave.) There it is, Dave. Take good care of it.

DAVE

I shall, Mrs. Valkonen. But it may be a long
time before I can deliver it.

MIRANDA

It will be a long time before my grandchild
learns to read.

DAVE (*after a moment's silence*)

I—I have to be going now . . . (*He goes quickly
to* UNCLE WALDEMAR.) Good-bye, Mr. Sederstrum.

UNCLE WALDEMAR (*shaking hands with* DAVE)
Good-bye, Mr. Corween.

MIRANDA

You'll surely let us know if you're going to
Stockholm?

DAVE

Oh, yes, Mrs. Valkonen.

MIRANDA

We'll miss you very much, Dave. You've really
become part of our life here in Helsinki.

(MIRANDA *and* DAVE *have gone out on that.*
UNCLE WALDEMAR *looks after them, then he sits
down at the piano. Still looking toward the door,
he starts to play the Finnish folk song heard at
the end of the first scene. After a moment,* MI-
RANDA *returns. She goes to the couch, and sits*

down where she had sat beside KAARLO. *She listens to* UNCLE WALDEMAR'S *playing. She looks to the left, where* ERIK *had been, and to the right, where* KAARLO *had been. She leans backward, wearily, and looks at nothing.* UNCLE WALDEMAR *goes on playing the tinkly little tune. There is a kind of peace in this Finnish-American house.)*

CURTAIN

THE END

WITHDRAWN